Christmas Carl

Merry Exmas Book 1

Alex Silver

Contents

SYNOPSIS:

CARL:

When my best friend suggests I get a fake holidate for a party, I laugh it off. There's no way my nosy family would buy the lie, and I've been ghosted by too many Mr. Wrongs to have any faith in finding the right guy. But then I run into Nick—literally—and replacing my spilled cocoa turns into flirting and a promise to make all my romantic holiday dreams come true. But only for a week.

Nick:

When my mom breaks her hip, I have to take a step back from my demanding career. I never expected her adorable boss to sweep me off my feet in a whirlwind fake Christmas romance, but I'm hooked from our first magical kiss. Every wonderful date with Carl has me questioning my life, and the love I've never given myself the chance to chase. Can the magic of Christmas turn a convenient lie into lasting love?

Christmas Carl is an M/M low-angst fake dating small-town Christmas romance between two ace men with a holiday market meet cute. It's the first book in the Merry Exmas duology, but both books can stand alone.

Chapter 1

CARL—DECEMBER 18TH

"So, HOW WAS YOUR date last night?" Saint asks, as though he's been waiting to spring the question on me all day. Maybe he has. I sign into the fitness center and head for the lockers, avoiding the question for as long as possible, for all the good that will do me.

My best friend and ex-husband follows me as I enter the locker room. Like a dog with a bone, as usual. I snort to myself, because I doubt Saint's ever met a bone he didn't like, and he's got a stubborn streak a kilometer wide.

"Well?" he asks, leaning against my locker.

"It was fine. Until he invited me back to his place for 'coffee.'" I turn to face him as I hook my fingers into air quotes.

"Oh." Saint's face falls, his broad grin turning into a frown. "Was there not coffee?"

"Nope, apparently I was supposed to realize 'coffee' meant sex, and going on five whole dates constitutes being more than patient enough when it comes to waiting for sex. Who knew?"

"I'm sorry, Carl. You two seemed to hit it off so well."

"Yeah. Well, he hasn't texted me back since. So I think it's over." I shrug and wrench open my locker to get changed. Saint claps me on the back so I'll turn for a proper hug.

"I'm sorry it didn't work out," he murmurs. Then he drops the subject and we both get changed for our usual workout.

It's not the first time I've broken up with a guy over my lack of interest in sex; I doubt it will be the last. There was a time when that bothered me more. When I tried desperately to change.

"So, how was your weekend?" I ask as I grab my water bottle, heading out to warm up, Saint follows, giving me a vague rendition of his weekend plans and then pivoting to some show he watched last night. Ah. So he probably had company this weekend. We don't talk about his active sex life most of the time.

I spent years, even after breaking up with Saint, where I hated that loving him with all my heart didn't somehow magically make me love sex with him.

It's not that the sex with him didn't feel good. It was fine. Perfectly adequate. Messier than taking care of myself in the shower, but fine. Except, I'd wanted to feel all those euphoric highs I'd read about in my older sister's romance novels. I wanted it to be this transcendent soul-deep

4

connection with another person. Some sort of spiritual experience or something. I wanted to look at him and feel that unquenchable desire. Just like in those books.

I never did. I've never felt that way about anyone. For the longest time, I thought it meant I was broken.

I jump into a few gentle stretches before hitting the weights. Saint follows my lead, putting our conversation on pause as we get our heart rates up.

We got married young, and it didn't take Saint long to realize something was wrong. He badgered me into admitting I don't really care for sex. And he was more mad about me forcing myself to do something I wasn't into than he was about not having sex as often.

Still, we weren't good for each other as partners. He's my best friend and getting a divorce a year into our marriage was the best thing we ever did. We were still in university, and it was a spur-of-the-moment marriage, fueled mostly by the giddy joy of finally being allowed to get married once it was legal. Our relationship shifted after that. It got deeper because I knew I could trust him with anything.

"You too distracted to spot me?" Saint arches a brow at me. I shake off my revelry and force a smile.

"I've got you," I say, rolling my shoulders. I will always have his back, the same way he's always had mine. Even when it hurt us both to admit we couldn't meet all of each other's needs.

The first time Saint plopped a romance book about an ace character in front of me, I cried at seeing someone who felt the same as me. At seeing someone like me who wasn't damaged or wrong. The character got to have a big sappy romance that didn't center around sex and it was perfect.

So that's what I'm holding out for when I go on dates. Not someone who is willing to settle for me, but someone who loves me with or without sex being part of the equation. It was funny, because as we read more about asexuality, Saint discovered himself too. He's aromantic, so we couldn't have been less compatible in that department if we tried, since romance does it for me. As friends, though, we're perfect. He's still my platonic life partner. I just want that romantic connection with a boyfriend too. It's probably too much to ask, judging from my abysmal dating track record.

"You going to try the apps again?" Saint asks as we head toward the free weights to do some circuit training.

"I'm not sure."

"You can't give up, man. How else am I going to get out of alimony?"

I guffaw. "Sorry, Saint. Guess you'll just have to keep me in the manner to which I am accustomed forever." I wink at him.

He doesn't actually have to pay me alimony. We were only married for about a year. Once we realized that we wanted different things from our marriage, we got a quiet divorce. But we still lived together as roommates for the better part of his time in law school after our separation became official.

He needed help around the house to get through his rigorous studies and I was happy with our arrangement as I established myself in my career after undergrad. My job paid the bills and kept us both in ramen. So he insisted on supporting me after law school, at least until we both got on our feet financially.

After he passed the bar, we sold our condo in Toronto—gifted to us by his parents when we got married because even in the early aughts, Toronto real estate was absurdly expensive—and bought a duplex back in our hometown of Elk's Pass, Ontario together. And Saint offered me eight years of spousal support or until I get with someone else, whichever comes first.

That was seven years ago, but every month he still puts a portion of his income into the joint account we never got around to closing. Every month I tell him I can't take his money. So he's got quite the nest egg growing there. If he really wanted to get out of the payments, he could stop. 'Getting out of alimony' is Saint code for 'I'm a big sap who wants my best friend to be happy, even if it's not with me.'

He loves me. And I love him, but there's no romance there. No spark.

We stretch and take turns spotting each other and I ignore my dating woes for a little while, intent on counting reps and enjoying the time being Saint's focus. He lives right next door, but I always appreciate our quality time together. After we've worked up a sweat, we typically go out for drinks.

But tonight, Saint grabs my arm and hauls me across the street to the quaint little Elk's Pass Christmas Market set up in the town square. Main Street is icy and lit up with LED snowflakes hanging off all the streetlights. Holiday displays are lit in practically every storefront. The uniform booths of the Christmas market across the street are bursting with a riot of colorful decorations and a bounty of local artisan crafts. They sell everything from clothing to snacks.

"No!" I protest through a laugh. "Saint, it's a week before Christmas. The market is going to be packed!"

"Yeah, but I still have to find the perfect ornament for Eliza's party on Saturday."

"You haven't gotten one yet? I bought mine ages ago. It's a cute little mouse in a tutu. Can't you have your secretary order something?"

"For your sister's big party? No, I can't. You know it has to be something special or else what's the point? I can't win the ornament swap with something mass produced."

I roll my eyes. "Um, you can't 'win' an ornament swap, Saint. It's not a competition."

"Ha, you sweet, naïve soul, that's what you think. There is always a winner. A best ornament of the swap that everyone wants to bring home as soon as they see it. Your cousin Oliver won last year and I will not be defeated again. Come on!" Saint tugs on my arm and levels me with his most irresistibly adorable pouty face.

"God, you know I can't resist the puppy eyes. No fair." I put up a final token resistance, shoving his face away.

Saint bats his big blue eyes at me, smiling against my fingers. "Please? Help me find the perfect Christmas ornament for your sister's party, Carl? Pretty please with sprinkles on top?" he lifts his clasped hands toward me in supplication, the big dork.

"Ugh! You're impossible." I can't hide my smile at his over-the-top charming antics. "Fine. Let's go find you the winning ornament."

"Yes!" Saint pumps his fist and whoops in triumph. Then he grabs my hand to cross the road, plunging us both into Christmas-themed chaos. Interlaced webs of garlands and lights hang between the array of craft booths, lighting everything in a festive glow as the bustling crowd of holiday shoppers swallows us whole.

Chapter 2

NICK—DECEMBER 18TH

STANDING IN THE MIDDLE of a craft booth at the Elk's Pass Holiday Market is not where I expected to be the week before Christmas. For one, I rarely venture back to my hometown these days. For another, the kitschy yarn crafts ranging from felt garland in nature-themed earthtones to rainbow hued crocheted hats and everything in between that I'm here to sell are as far from the sleek modern stylings of my condo as it is possible to get. But they're my mother's work so I catch myself beaming with pride every time a customer coos over the art on display.

Strangers appreciating her work makes me glad I let Mom convince me to run the booth instead of spending the extra time with her. If she had canceled at the last minute, she would have lost the prestigious slot it took her years to secure. I can see why, with the constant stream of customers filing past. There are more people than I'd have thought possible, considering Elk's Pass doesn't have a huge population. The market draws tourists from nearby Niagara Falls this time of year.

Returning home to Elk's Pass, Ontario, when I found out my mom needed surgery was the hardest decision I ever made, even if it is temporary. I have a life in Toronto; friends, an apartment I barely see, a job I don't hate most of the time, and a favorite coffee shop along my morning commute. My ever-growing bank account almost makes up for my utter lack of free time. Not to mention a string of failed relationships.

I make a mental note that I need to replenish the cute little display tree with more Mom's felt gnome ornaments. They've been particularly popular this season. I can see why; they're adorable. You can see the love Mom pours into every piece. She's always been generous with her love, even when I don't make the time that I should to spend with her.

I haven't been home for the holidays in ages, but Mom needed me this year. I've told her and her best friend Beatrice for years not to rollerblade on the road for their morning constitutional. So I was mostly relieved that she wasn't hurt worse when she tripped over someone's badly placed trash when she was showing off her fancy footwork. It could have been so much worse, but the need for major orthopedic surgery took us both by surprise. Even though she was older than most of my peers' parents growing up, she's always lived life to the fullest. I don't like thinking my mom isn't indestructible.

So no matter how inconvenient the timing is, I'm not heartless enough to leave her in the lurch as she recovers from her hip replacement. It was either move home to help her out or put her in one of those facilities while she recovered. With all the horror stories I read about those sorts of places when I looked into our options—not to mention the ridiculous price tag—it quickly became obvious that I needed to take a leave of absence to be here for her.

Even if being here for her means tidying up the hats she's got on display after a young couple tries on a dozen of them and leaves them in disarray once they settle on a matching pair.

My boss, Jim, isn't thrilled that I'm out of the office, and I've fielded several calls asking when I'll be back and requesting quick remote projects. Jim's not used to me saying no to any amount of overtime. Mom's not wrong when she says that I work too much, but I always figured she only said that because she wants me to visit more. It never registered until now that she's getting older and I might have a limited number of Christmases left to spend with her.

I agreed to wrap up some loose ends for a big campaign remotely to get the time off. I didn't count on needing to take over the craft booth. Mom tried to insist that she could manage the booth on her own with a stool. Tough as she is, there is no way she could be on her feet or even sitting out in the cold for hours on end each day less than a month out from a major surgery. So I had no choice but to handle her craft business for her as a compromise. Between the market and helping Mom around the house, it took me until this past weekend to submit the final files to Jim. We're down to the wire if the client requests any more last-minute corrections on their boxing day social media ad blitz.

I'm exhausted from pulling double duty, but this is what I signed up for when I agreed to handle everything for Mom during her recovery. And the reminder of her mortality has me feeling guilty for all the years of putting my job over our relationship. At least she's organized.

Mom had everything for her annual market stall packed up and ready to go, complete with a diagram of how to set up her booth. She even called me for regular video-chat check-ins to micromanage my progress as I was setting up her stall.

Mom's made her little art pieces for as long as I can remember, but it wasn't until she retired that she started to actually sell her work. Now she stays busy with a part-time reception job with a local nonprofit, and her crafts. All of her art is selling well. I've lost count of the number of people who remark that they're here for a unique gift idea.

I'm just glad the market has a complementary wrapping booth staffed by volunteer elves. My wrapping skills are not up to the number of requests for gift wrap that I've gotten.

The whimsical forest creature tree ornaments that she spent months making by the score are still selling like hotcakes. I've barely had time to restock the table with all the sales. So I'm down to a final pair of kissing gnomes on the little display stand tree when two customers reach for the ornament at the same time.

Oooh boy. The last thing I need is a holiday hoopla over the last felted gnome ornament on the tree. I should have hung up a few more of them after I sold a dozen to a frazzled mom with two toddlers in tow, but business has been steady. The felted gnomes of all sizes, with their crocheted outfits, have been among Mom's most popular wares so far.

"I saw it first!" one man exclaims.

"Back off, bucko, this is my winning ornament!" The other tugs.

Visions of the ornament tearing in their rough grasps have me picturing Mom's disappointment. She puts so much love into each one of her designs.

"May I help you gentlemen to find something?" I step in, hoping to diffuse the situation before it escalates beyond an impromptu tug-of-war.

"Babe, let it go, he was here first," the second guy's companion—from the endearment, I'm guessing his boyfriend—cajoles, tugging at his sleeve.

"But it's perfect for the ornament swap," the boyfriend growls, yanking harder.

I wince.

"Hey, I'll have to charge you both for it if it breaks!" I interject. That gives the squabbling pair pause. "I do have other ornaments that aren't on display yet. Perhaps you'd like to see the others?" I cajole, sensing that they can be swayed.

"I need this ornament to replace the one we got from our son before he passed. Our cat knocked over the tree and then our dog got hold of the kissing gnomes. My wife will be devastated if I can't replace it before she realizes what happened. Please?" The man's heartfelt request only partially sways the other man. He loosens his grip. His partner elbows him hard, and he reluctantly releases his grip on the gnomes.

"Sorry for your loss," the boyfriend says.

"Thank you. Can you ring me up?" The customer asks, clutching the gnome ornament to his chest. I swipe his card, wrap the ornament in tissue and slide it carefully into a protective box. The man takes the ornament and his receipt and bustles away.

The couple are browsing Mom's other work when I overhear the one who wanted the ornament grumbling. They intrigue me, the contrast between them keeps drawing my gaze. The grumbly one is a buttoned up silver fox in fashionable winter coat and a muted plaid scarf, the other is a burly bearded bear of a man with a purple and teal hat and scarf combo that reminds me of Mom's wares.

"How much do you want to bet he made up the sob story?" Silver Fox asks.

His boyfriend gives him a sharp look. "Really?"

"What? People lie all the time, Carl."

"Glad to know you still see the best in people, Saint. Santa's watching, you know."

"I'm perfectly happy on Santa's naughty list, babe." Saint, the one with the model-good looks, winks flirtatiously.

Carl flushes and shoves at his partner. He's adorable, with his round, bearded cheeks and sweet faith in humanity. "Stop trying to bait me. We still have to find the perfect ornament."

"True." Saint turns toward me. "You were saying you have more?"

"I do." I rummage under the table for the plastic tote with more of the gnome ornaments in assorted designs. At this rate, there might not be enough to last through the rest of the week until Christmas Eve. But I know Mom has some more at home. "Mom also takes custom orders, but she's got so many already. I'm not sure it would be ready in time if you need it for a party."

"Wait." Carl steps back and looks at Mom's sign. Tina's Tiny Creations. "I knew the style looked familiar! Your mom is Tina Tremblay, right? You're Nick?"

"You know my mom?" I ask, and then I could kick myself, because of course he knows her. It's not like Elk's Pass is a bustling metropolis. From a rough estimate of his age, I probably went to school with this guy, maybe a few years ahead of him. Everyone knows everyone here. "And yeah, I'm Nick, lovely to meet a friend of Mom's."

"I do. She works with my organization. She was thrilled to have you home for the holidays this year. How is she holding up? I bet she's raring to get back on her feet ASAP, huh?"

"You *do* know Mom," I say with a chuckle. "She's recovering as well as can be expected. Like you said, the hardest part is getting her to take it easy and not strain herself."

"Well, I'm glad you were able to come and help her out. She was worried about missing the holiday market this year. I'm so happy her work is still here, even though she can't be. Pass along my regards?"

"Of course..." I trail off to let him introduce himself officially.

"Oh, Carl. Carl Meadows. And this is Mathieu Saint John. Everyone calls him Saint though."

"Charmed, darling." Saint extends his hand toward me in greeting.

I catch the none-too-subtle way he's eye-fucking me. I can't quite keep the disapproval off my face at him doing that in front of his...whatever Carl is to him. Sure, I might be a shitty boyfriend most of the time, but I've never blatantly tried to hit on someone in front of my exes. Saint grins at me and wraps an arm around Carl's shoulders.

"Ah, this isn't what you're thinking. Despite the endearments, you'll be pleased to know Carl here is very much my ex and both of us are very single." He bats his lashes at me.

Ex. His ex? I blink at the two of them in confusion. They seem awfully chummy for exes. But then again, not everyone has an explosive scorched-earth-style breakup like I did with my college boyfriend. He burned my stuff on his front lawn. I've learned to avoid drama since Teddy.

"Nice to meet you, Carl and Saint." I shake their hands.

There's something about Carl's smile—and all the stories Mom has told me about how kind he is—that makes me linger over his hand. His calloused fingers are warm in my grasp. When our eyes meet, I could get lost in those gorgeous brown depths.

Plenty of people get along just fine with their exes. Not me. Most of my exes leave acrimoniously after one too many missed dates and canceled plans. My track record is bleak when it comes to staying in touch while we're together, let alone after it ends. I work long hours and that takes a toll on any relationship. I've always chalked it up to the cost of success.

My most recent breakup with Timothy happened last month. I told him I was taking a leave of absence to go home and help my mom and that I wouldn't be back until after the holidays. He kept hinting about coming with me. I didn't take the bait.

"I've heard so much about you both from Mom," I say. That's the truth. Mom has talked my ear off about 'the nice young man' who runs the drop-in center for the elderly where she works part time these days. The nice, young—emphasis on the single—gay man. It hits me like a bolt of understanding that she talks so much about Carl for a reason. Has she been trying to play matchmaker? Impossible.

Timothy only just broke things off with me. He kept hinting about taking care of my place for me while I was gone, maybe making some updates to the decor. Turns out I didn't realize he was angling to move things to the next level by moving in together and meeting the family. The longer it took me to figure out what was behind his sudden interest in my mom's health, the more snippy and passive aggressive he got with me.

When I finally confronted him about it, he spelled it all out. He was so exasperated with me and I never got the memo that he wanted more than I had to offer him with my busy work schedule. Toward the end, he expected me to pick up the tab for everything and every date ended in sex, no matter how tired I was from work.

"All good, I'm sure." Saint pats Carl on the back, then he winks at me. It takes me a second to parse that he means the things Mom's been saying. "This guy is a catch."

Huh. That's weird right? Trying to set your ex up on a date? It's oddly endearing, even though I'm in no position to be thinking about dating again.

It's possible I'm not dating material. I certainly wasn't ready to 'move things to the next level' with Timothy when I wasn't even happy at our existing level. I can't blame him. Not when I didn't feel the same things for him that he clearly felt for me. His dumping me was for the best. I don't have room in my life for a sex-obsessed boyfriend who seems more interested in spending my money than spending time together. I have even less room to be best buds with an ex.

But Carl and Saint seem to be close, even just perusing Mom's booth as I reach under the display table for the box of extra ornaments. They make each other smile despite whatever differences broke them up, and I can't deny a part of me longs for that sort of teasing friendship with someone. Not that I'm going to find it here, of all places.

I clear my throat and hold up the plastic tote full of ornaments for Saint's perusal. He grins and reaches immediately for a large gnome with a fluffy white beard and a jaunty rainbow striped hat. The ornament has a little Christmas tree slung over his shoulder.

"Look! It's perfect."

"So meta, the tree ornament holding a tree." Carl touches the ornament's beard fluff with one finger. "That's the one, right?"

Saint nods firmly. "This is what a winning ornament looks like, handcrafted by a local artisan, kitschy-cool without being too much, you know? Plus, his little hat is fab. How much?" That last is directed at me, and from the way Carl is smiling at me, I'm half tempted to tell Saint there's no charge. But I'm running my mom's business, so I quote him the actual price.

Saint pays without haggling. A surprising number of Mom's customers here seem to be bargain hunters. She told me she builds wiggle room into her price sheet for those sorts of negotiations when I complained. It's not what I'm used to, but I've been finding I enjoy the market. There's something special about seeing people fall in love with Mom's hard work.

The way Saint cradles the little rainbow ornament in his hands like a treasure warms my heart. I wave the duo away from my stall and turn to answer a question from a browser who is looking over some of Mom's bigger pieces. Business is booming. I push the cute former couple to the back of my mind and get back to hawking Mom's wares.

Chapter 3

CARL—DECEMBER 18TH

"HE WAS CUTE." SAINT nudges me with an elbow as we leave Tina's booth—and her son—behind us.

"What?" I glance around, as though Nick might overhear us. "You mean the guy you acted like a belligerent child in front of? Why do the holidays make you act a decade younger?"

Saint snorts. "Darling, we're in our thirties; I'm acting at least two decades younger. If you can't let out your inner child for Christmas, then when can you?"

"Sure. Right. Makes perfect sense," I say dryly, but Saint is only half paying attention. He grabs my arm, squeezing just a bit too hard as he points toward a stall a few yards away.

"Cocoa! Come on, Carl, we have to get some."

"We really don't," I protest. But he's already dragging me to join the disproportionately long line to the booth run by a local dairy farmer. Saint happily narrates the entire menu to me.

"I think I'm going to get the white chocolate peppermint. You know they make it with real chocolate, right?"

"Yes."

"Stop looking so dour. It's Christmas, babe."

"It's December, but Christmas is still a week away." I don't add that all the magic was gone the first time I woke up alone in my half of the duplex on Christmas morning. I didn't realize that our divorce hadn't quite felt real until I had to figure out how to live without him. We still share a wall and a close friendship, but this way there's enough separation for me to let go of the idea we can fulfill each other's relationship needs.

My folks had all kinds of traditions growing up. And Saint and I made our own traditions while we were together. We kept them up over his years of law school, when we were living together. But we let most of them fall by the wayside since moving back to our hometown. I just couldn't handle facing our traditions alone.

We're still neighbors, but each of us has our own townhouse. Two condos in a duplex. We wanted to stay close. Saint has been my best friend forever and our divorce didn't change that.

I firmly believe we work better as friends than lovers, but there are times when I miss what we tried to build together. A special person to curl up next to and share the anticipation of a big event. Someone to romance and who wants to woo me in return.

Truthfully, I'm dreading all the family-centric holiday gatherings that are bound to remind me just how alone I am. Sure, I've got Saint, but I want... not more, but different. Someone who is happy to cuddle in my bed without it going further. Someone who can kiss me under the mistletoe without expecting it to lead to more.

I long to meet someone who smiles at me the way Nick smiled, and it felt like time slowed and everything else was in soft focus. I shake off the absurd thought. Nick was just trying to make a sale. He wasn't into me.

Even if a guy who drops everything to come help his ailing mother with her craft business is exactly my type. That last might be a stretch, considering Nick hasn't been home in years. It took Tina needing major surgery for him to return home for the holidays, but he's here when it counts, right?

While I'm daydreaming, the line moves and Saint nudges me out of my thoughts to order.

"Same as him," I say. The menu is too long to panic-read it while I hold up the long line of holiday shoppers.

Saint scoffs. "No, he'll have the salted caramel dark chocolate with extra whip," he corrects my order. And that does sound better than white chocolate peppermint. The person behind the counter gives me a questioning look, and I nod.

"Yeah, what he said, salted caramel dark chocolate, please." I pay for us both and we step aside to wait for our orders.

"Hmm, distracted, huh?" Saint jostles me with his elbow.

"Mhm."

Saint grins. "That wouldn't have anything to do with a certain craft merchant, would it?"

"Nope. Not at all. Just dreading going to Eliza's party."

"Why? Your sister's party is pretty much the highlight of the season. You used to love it."

"Yeah. Except I'll be the only single sibling again this year. And since Gail is pregnant, I won't even get a reprieve where the rest of the family speculates over when she and Marcus are going to start producing grandchildren. I mean, I adore my family, but they are nosy."

"And the baby won't be enough to keep their attention?"

I shrug. "Sure, but they like to meddle."

"So, find a date to bring."

"Why do you think I've been trying the apps again? But it's getting a bit short notice to spring a 'meet the family' holiday party on a new love interest."

"You could try to find someone who needs a similar holiday boyfriend to throw off the nosy family. Swap fake holidates?" Saint suggests. I roll my eyes.

"Because the only thing better than lying to and disappointing one family is doing the same to two families?" I snipe.

The worst part would be that I'd want so desperately for it not to be a lie that the night would be torture. Twice the torture. And desperately wanting more from something that isn't good for me has never turned out well. Our marriage being the case-in-point for that.

Saint bumps our shoulders and flashes me a conspiratorial grin. "Worst case, we could pretend to get back together."

I'm struck speechless at all the many ways in which that's a terrible idea. Before I can say so, our orders are ready. Saint winks at me as he collects both cups. He passes mine to me.

"We aren't doing that."

"Okay." Saint shrugs laconically, sipping his cocoa and moaning into the steam.

"I don't need a fake date. Are you trying to make my life into a Hallmark movie or something?"

"Of course not, babe."

"More like something off unsolved mysteries, knowing my dating skills," I grumble.

Saint elbows me. "Don't even joke about that. I want out of alimony, but not that bad."

I roll my eyes at him again. "You still don't owe me alimony, Saint."

"Details." He waves away my protest, eyes scanning the market for our next stop. "Come on, let's walk by Hotty McHotness's booth again."

Before I can protest, he seizes my arm and pulls me back through the holiday throngs toward the craft booth. Knowing Saint, he'll find some excuse to shove me toward Nick's booth before remembering something urgent in the opposite direction. That's just the sort of incorrigible meddling that makes him my best friend.

Chapter 4

NICK—DECEMBER 18TH

WITH FREQUENT INTERRUPTIONS FROM customers, it takes me quite a while to finish restocking the little fake tree with Mom's ornaments. It's the sort of problem I'm sure she'll be happy for me to report having. The market's hours are coming to a close by the time I finish and my sales wind down as the crowd thins.

I start closing everything down for the night as I see my neighbors to either side shuttering their sturdy little wooden booths. I follow their lead, getting ready to do the same. First, I make sure Mom's wares are tidy and ready for when we reopen tomorrow. Then I pack up a few of the more valuable small pieces and the money box to bring home for the night.

When everything matches the diagram Mom gave me for closing procedures, I grab my bag and sling the strap over one shoulder. Then I go around to the front of the booth to lock up. It takes a little finagling to secure the heavy wooden shutters over the booth for the night. Most of the other vendors are also locking up, but a few shoppers are trying to squeeze in last-minute purchases. I'm sure that will only get worse the closer we get to the actual holiday.

I get distracted, fighting with a stuck shutter. When it suddenly comes loose, I stumble back, and right into someone. I have an apology on the tip of my tongue as hands close around my biceps to steady me.

"Sorry I..." I trail off as I gaze over my shoulder into kind brown eyes. It's Carl. Mom's boss at the Days of Grace drop-in center. All the times she's mentioned him to me did not prepare me for the compassion in his warm gaze. He steadies me and keeps me from falling on my ass in the snow.

"Whoa! That was a close one," Carl says, still supporting me, even though I've had ample time to recover my footing. "You alright?"

"Fine," I say, taking his cue to straighten up and stop leaning on him. I miss his steadying closeness immediately.

Carl smiles at me, and it's as warm as the hands still squeezing my arms. It's reassuring, this moment of contact with a stranger. I'm struck with the sudden urge to not let him walk away again. Then I catch sight of his dropped cup sporting the distinctive logo from the fancy hot cocoa booth further inside the market.

"Oh no. I'm sorry about your hot chocolate." I gesture to the fallen cup. "Did I make you drop it?"

"Nah, it's fine; I was almost done, anyway."

The sludgy puddle of melted snow and cocoa by his feet belies his words. And just like that, I have a plan to keep this man's attention for a little while longer. The craft booths are closing, but usually the food and beverage vendors near the big skating rink in the central square stay open longer. They cater to the post-skating rush, since the ice is open for a few more hours.

"Let me buy you a replacement?" I offer.

Carl bites his lip. "It's really alright, you don't have to do that."

"I want to," I insist, and then it occurs to me that I shouldn't bulldoze over him if he really doesn't want to get a drink with me. "I mean, I can give you cash to get a new one, if you'd prefer. But I'd love to treat us both to a drink? Like a date?" I offer him my hand, letting myself get swept up in the holiday atmosphere and a sweet smile.

"You would?" Carl looks taken aback, but then he flashes me a shy grin that makes my heart flutter. "I'd like that very much, Nick. Thank you."

He tentatively takes my offered hand and I lead him through the warren of closing stalls. We join the long line.

"They sure stay busy," Carl says, shooting me a nervous glance. "We don't have to—"

I shake my head. "I want to. The long line just means I get you to myself a little longer." I grin and squeeze his hand.

Carl flashes me another of his gorgeous smiles. "If you're sure."

"Very sure. Do you know what flavor you want?"

"Oh, yeah. I'm boring. I always get the same thing. Salted caramel dark chocolate with extra whip."

"Mm, that sounds good." And it does. I can already imagine tasting that flavor on his lips when we kiss—and I'm getting way ahead of myself.

"Not boring at all. I think I'll have the same." How can he think he's boring?

Carl grins at me. "It is good. Reminds me of my favorite chocolate bars. Have you had their cocoa before?"

"Not yet. I usually can't get much time off around the holidays with my job. It's a busy time of year for advertising."

"That must be hard. I'm sure Tina is thrilled to have you around this year."

"It's been good to have more quality time together while she's recovering, yeah. Don't tell her, or I'll never hear the end of it, but I might just miss this little town when I go back to Toronto next month." I angle myself closer to him and make the statement almost conspiratorial.

Carl leans in, mirroring me, and is it just my imagination or does he seem disappointed at the reminder I'm going back to the city after the holidays? Wishful thinking, I'm sure.

"Ah, she'll miss you. But my lips are sealed. Miss Tina is not one to let go of an idea easily."

"She is not. Mom says this cocoa is as good as it smells walking by, so I'm sure we're in for a treat." I don't just mean the drinks. There's something about this man that calls to me. It's in his bright smile and the way he drinks in all the festive sights of the market with a delighted gleam in his eyes. He's joyful.

"She's right." Carl nods.

"She almost always is." I wink at him. "She told me I'd like you."

Carl glances away, as though flirting makes him uncomfortable. "You barely know me."

"Fair, so let's fix that. Tell me what I should know about you."

"Really?" Carl snorts in amusement. "This isn't a job interview—" Carl stops abruptly, bites his lip, gives his head a shake and then turns to me with a rueful smile. "Actually, this is probably a ridiculous idea, but what would you say to being my boyfriend for the day?"

"Um, explain?" I say, taken aback at the sudden escalation.

"Well, my sister, Eliza and her wife, have this huge holiday party every year. And ever since Saint and I got divorced, the entire family seems to be on my case to find someone new. They think I'm still hung up on him, even though what we had is ancient history. I know they mean well, but it's hard enough being single for the holidays without them putting more pressure on me, you know? Anyway, he was joking about finding me a fake date. Standing here with you, I can't help thinking it would be nice for them not to focus on my failed love life for once. I figure, if I bring you, they'll lay off. And then I can tell them we broke up after the holidays when you go back to Toronto."

"Ah, the old fake boyfriend gambit? You think it will work?"

"Sure. I don't see why they'd question it; you're exactly my type."

"Charming and debonair?" I tease, striking a pose. I saw his ex and the two of us don't look at all alike. Saint was impeccably dressed, all lean elegance, ice-blue eyes, striking features, and distinguished salt and pepper hair. I'm plain by comparison. Brown hair, brown eyes, soft around the middle from long hours at my desk.

Carl laughs and shoves at my shoulder. "Sure, we'll go with that instead of admitting I have a track record of falling for self-assured workaholics who don't have time for love."

"Ouch." I clutch at my chest as though he's struck a mortal blow. "You wound me, sir. Has Mom been telling tales?"

Carl rolls his eyes. "Almost forgot to add silly goofballs to that list. And your mother is very proud of how hard you work. I was more referring to my dating history."

"So, I really am your type?" I press.

Before he can answer, we get to the front of the line and place our orders. I whip out my card to pay. Carl thanks me and tucks a few bills into the tip jar for us. Which is a nice change from my usual dates, who are all too willing to let me foot the bill wherever we go.

Carl sidles closer to me as we wait for our orders. "I want to show you something. You know, since you're new to the market."

"I'd love to see anything you want to show me." I let my gaze wander over his body, hidden under bulky winter clothing. From his full beard and broad frame, I suspect he's a bit of a hairy bear. I know he's strong from the way he held me up earlier. Rather than flirting back, Carl leans away from me at the innuendo, eyes not meeting mine. Well, I apparently read that wrong, but he still seems interested. I'll just have to take this slower and follow his lead. "What did you have in mind?"

"You'll see. I mean, you might've seen it already, since you're working here at your mom's booth. I just...it's silly, just forget I said anything." He bites his lips, and I shove away the fantasy of kissing him.

"No, I'm sure it's not silly at all. Tell me, Carl." I pout at him.

He rolls his eyes, then takes a deep breath and nods. "Fine, but remember, you asked for it. They put up an enormous tree and decorate it with all sorts of lights and balls and things, and there's a skating rink all around it. I've always thought all the couples skating together under the lights seem very romantic."

"Let's go try it, then." I offer him my hand as they call out our orders.

We get our drinks. Carl twines the fingers of our free hands as we walk along the main corridor of the market. We stroll under strings of twinkling holiday lights, all the way to the huge, decorated tree at the center of the market.

We stand together, gazing up at the tree, faces lit by the muted glow of the decorations. He looks so lovely in that hazy golden light as he sips his drink, a bit of whipped cream stuck in his bushy hipster beard. I'm tempted to pull him in and kiss away the mess. I can see exactly what he meant when he called this spot romantic. The soft ambiance makes him seem otherworldly, a warm contrast to the ice and snow on every surface.

As soft fluffy flakes of snow start sifting down from the darkened sky, I can almost convince myself that anything we do together can be a moment away from reality. A magical moment frozen in time where I can be the guy someone relies on instead of the workaholic who barely sees his penthouse apartment enough to keep his houseplants alive.

I'm not that guy. My ficus was a dead husk well before I left town to help Mom. Our clients pay astronomical sums to get their ads in front of prospective clients and it's a competitive industry, especially starting out. Everyone I know puts in ridiculous overtime and it seems normal until I spend time outside my work bubble and realize other people have lives. Partners they actually get to spend time with. Gazing into Carl's eyes, surrounded by the magic of the holiday season, part of me wants to be someone entirely different.

Not an absentee son, but one my mother can be proud to introduce to the people in her life. Not the unreliable boyfriend who always has something work-related come up last minute to cancel all our best laid plans. The sort of man Carl deserves to have holding his hand as he skates around the tree and goes to his family's big party. And maybe I can't be that person for real, but Carl offered me a chance to pretend. To play that role for the next week.

"Hey, Carl?"

"Yeah?" He tears his gaze away from the enormous tree and the skating couples and gives me a questioning look.

"Let's do it."

"It?" Carl's voice goes up an octave at the question. "Do *what* exactly?"

"Let's be fake boyfriends until I have to go home. I've missed all the magic of the season too—so, why not? We can do the entire over-the-top song and dance. Matching Christmas Eve pajama selfies, skating in the park, his-and-his ugly sweaters for the party. Pull out all the stops."

"Just to be clear, I was only suggesting we pretend for the party, but it sounds like you want to, what? Make a list of all the holiday traditions couples do and pretend?"

"Yeah. You said you missed it and I do too. Plus, it will make our act more believable for the party. So why not?"

Carl splutters for a moment, but then he nods. "Yeah. Okay. We'll make a list."

"And check it twice." I grin at him.

"Pretty sure this makes us both naughty," Carl says.

"I'm alright with that, as long as you are." I nudge our shoulders together, glad of an excuse to get closer to him. He flashes me a grin.

"I am. Just one thing?" His smile fades to worry as he bites his lip.

"Yeah?"

"If we're doing this, I don't want there to be any confusion." Carl meets my gaze. "I don't do casual sex."

"Got it. Does that mean we have to skip kissing under the mistletoe?"

"Oh, kissing is fine. I'd classify that as romance, not sex." He rubs at his neck, as if talking about kissing flusters him, but from his smile, it's a good kind of flustered.

"Hmm, in that case, pucker up, baby." I point up to the wire-frame archway covered in holiday greenery that we're standing under. Someone hung a ball of mistletoe among the lights.

Carl follows my gaze, then he grins as he loops an arm around my neck. He pulls me into the sweetest kiss I've had in ages. His body presses against me as he clings to my neck and I open to his tongue. I let him lead as our lips meld and he floods my senses with desire.

Chapter 5

CARL—DECEMBER 18TH

My EYES FLUTTER OPEN, and I realize I'm not thinking clearly. I just kissed a relative stranger in the middle of the Christmas market. Not just any stranger, but Tina's workaholic son. Who almost never comes home to visit his aging mother because he's too busy chasing the almighty dollar. What am I thinking?

But then I gaze into Nick's warm caramel eyes, and I know exactly what I'm thinking. I want to be swept off my feet, even if it's not real. Nick is offering me the best chance I've got at a textbook perfect romantic holiday season. He's attractive and charming and best of all, I know there's no chance of this lasting past New Year's Eve. So there's no pressure for this to be something it's not. No weight of unspoken expectations.

Nick agreed to no sex, and he seems just as enthusiastic about having a holiday date as I am. We can keep my family off my back, and our hearts out of it, all while soaking up the romantic memories for when I'm alone again come January first. It's a foolproof plan.

"Mm. You okay?" Nick tips up my chin, noticing the nerves from my racing thoughts.

"Perfect." I smile at him, forcing my muscles to unclench.

"Good. Want to skate now?" Nick offers me his arm and I loop mine through his.

"Sure, come on, hopefully they still have rentals in our sizes." I tug him toward the kiosk where they sell tickets and skate rentals. I pay for two sets.

"I can get my own," Nick protests.

"You got our drinks, so it's only fair."

Nick beams at me as the attendant looks for our sizes. I'm rarely thankful for having small feet, but it pays off in situations like this. I get a pair of skates in my size, but Nick has to settle for skates a size and a half too large.

The booth attendant laughingly sells him an extra pair of handcrafted, thick wool holiday socks. An intrepid local vendor left them at the booth for this purpose. The thick wool seems like enough to pad out the difference, but Nick still wobbles on his feet after lacing the skates up.

I chuckle as he tries to balance and take his arm. "I've got you, babe. Tell me you've at least skated before?"

The endearment slips out unbidden. It's flippant and mostly the result of spending so much time with Saint who throws around pet names with impunity. It feels a little disingenuous with someone I've just met, but if this plan is going to work I'll need to get used to calling Nick something sweet.

"Oh, sure. All the time." He waves his hand dismissively, but then he flashes me a sheepish grin, and I want to see more of it. "When I was twelve. It's been a few years since I made time for it."

I laugh. "Okay, well, I go every year around this time. Saint usually makes time to come out with a group of our friends at least once a season. I'll hold your hand."

Nick beams at me, his expression turning sly.

"Sounds like I should pretend not to remember how to do this for as long as possible, then." He winks. "You know, if it means I get to sidle up close to my baby."

My cheeks heat with the warm rush of being flirted with. It stirs up a blend of emotions. The giddy excitement of that first blush of a mutual attraction mixed with hope that he won't push for more, since we already discussed taking this slow. It's a rush to connect like this with someone so effortlessly, I already don't want it to end. I gulp my hot cocoa to hide my reaction, then nod toward his hand once I've got my flush under control. "Finish your drink so you don't spill it everywhere when we inevitably fall on our asses."

We both chug the last of our delicious drinks, and I take his cup to drop it in a bin nearby. Then I loop our arms together and we step onto the ice.

His feet immediately go out from under him, dragging me down with him in a heap. I glance over at him as the jolt of landing on my ass wears off, and I can't help but grin at his look of shock. He catches my eye and gives me a sheepish half-smile.

"Guess it's not like riding a bike, huh?" he jokes.

"Not quite." I get back up by rote, because even if I only go a few times a year these days, skating *is* as familiar as riding a bike to me. Moreso, considering our long winters and the lessons Eliza, Gail, and I used to take. We were all in every junior ice dance show from the time we could strap blades to our feet until we aged out of the program at the rec department. Eliza was good enough to consider serious competitions until a fall tore a ligament in her knee, but I was never as committed to the sport as my sister.

"Um, I might need help." Nick fumbles around, trying to get his feet under him. "How did I do this as a kid?"

"It helps that kids are fearless. Kneel first," I direct him, holding back my amusement. "Then plant one skate and push up off your thigh."

"Ah, so, like I'm proposing?" Nick flashes me a cheeky grin as he assumes the position. "Are you dropping hints for Christmas morning?"

My pulse pounds when Nick gazes up at me with all that intensity. It's like the rest of the world has faded into the background and we're the center of our own little universe. It's achingly similar to all my daydreams of a perfect love story. My heart races at how well the moment lives up to the fantasy. I try to ignore the way Nick's smile makes my emotions surge in my chest. There's something about him kneeling in front of me like this that's far too evocative, even coming from a fake boyfriend. It's suddenly too much, too vulnerable and raw. Too painful a reminder of what I wish I had for real.

"I don't do proposals until at least the fourth or fifth date. Here, I'll help you up." I grab his hand and haul him to his feet.

Nick barely totters stiffly away by about a meter before he hits a rut in the ice. His skate slips, body pitching in a vain effort to counterbalance, his arms windmilling. He barely keeps his feet and gives me a wide-eyed, imploring look. "I think I need help."

"Sure, I've got you." I skate backwards in front of Nick to steady him with both hands on his biceps, to keep him from toppling again. This time, when he pushes off, it goes a little better. Until a kid zips in front of me. I catch the movement in the corner of my eye, but that distracts me from Nick's response.

"Watch out!" Nick tries to stop, but he ends up digging in the toe picks on the rental skates, the momentum pitching him forward. At the back of my mind, I recognize that if he's like most of the guys I grew up with, he's probably more used to hockey skates with smooth blades. Well, crapola. It's like I'm watching the next few moments unfold as a bystander, helpless to do anything but take Nick's weight and not land on the kid behind me.

Nick skids into me. Our bodies collide. I wrap him in my arms and let his momentum spin us in a circle as I steady us both. The child darts away, oblivious to the brush with peril.

Nick clings to me, breathing hard, and for a heady moment, I'm holding another man in my arms as we whirl together in a tight half-spin. It reminds me of every fantasy I ever had about skating arm in arm with a lover when I was one of the only boys in my figure skating classes.

A snapshot moment out of a fantasy of how my storybook romance might unfold, and of course it's all pretend. I shake off the thought and let myself cling a little longer, revel in Nick's tight grip on the lapels of my jacket.

"Whoa! That was a close one," Nick says, breathless and smiling. Humor lights up his face. "My hero."

"You alright?" I ask, running my hands along his arms, taking comfort in the contact.

"Yeah, you better hold my hand to make sure I don't fall again, or crash into anyone else though." Nick offers me his gloved palm.

I release my grip on him to twine our fingers, and we take our first wobbling steps together, moving around the edge of the rink. I take it slow as the other skaters zip past us. Other couples glide hand-in-hand and laughing children dart between them. Nick almost falls a few more times on the first loop, he's so stiff on the ice. I'm not sure if he's hating this. But he doggedly gets back up and takes my hand following each stumble.

After the first few turns around the ice, Nick seems more comfortable on his feet. It's like the motions and balance really are coming back to him, but he doesn't relinquish my hand. I hold on to him too.

"I think I'm getting the hang of this, again." Nick offers me a shy smile as we complete another circuit without him falling.

"You are," I agree, then I turn to skate backwards, taking both of his hands and showing off a little to "Rockin' around the Christmas Tree".

Nick laughs when I skate ahead to end the song with a flourish. It's been ages since I met anyone who brought out this side of me. I whirl in a tight spin that leaves me a little dizzy at how good it feels to show off for a guy. And maybe a little because I forgot to spot the spin. I should try to get on the ice more often again. Our eyes meet and Nick's face lights up with delight as he claps. My breath catches at his open admiration as he skates painstakingly over to me, holding out his hand for me to take again.

"Bravo, babe. You're fantastic out here." His praise warms me to my toes as I clasp his hand and we skate close again.

Nick makes me feel playful and uninhibited. There's nothing to prove with the ending to this fake fling already written, so I can just be myself with him.

Nick grins over at me with a challenge in his eyes when "All I want for Christmas is You" plays over the loudspeakers. Bolder now, he skates a bit faster as he lip syncs the saccharine sweet words at me. As if he's really my boyfriend and I can really have this. Well, we've agreed that we can both have the perfect holiday season romance together, so I'm going to stop reminding myself it's fake and embrace every wonderful moment.

It's a perfect night and I feel like I've been transported to a place outside of time as we glide around the Christmas tree. Holiday music and the scents of fresh ice, pine, and cocoa fill the air. The twinkling lights lend everything a soft romantic glow. Through it all, Nick doesn't drop my hand. He holds on tight until the rink is closing and we have to turn in our skates.

As we're walking hand-in-hand back through the closed market, we pause again under the mistletoe. Nick's lips mold to mine like we've been doing this for far longer than one night. He kisses me with the ease of someone who's spent the past few hours with our bodies moving in sync on the ice. The perfect give and take of lips and tongue.

When we pull apart, Nick has a soft smile on his face. He brushes his finger along my jaw, tender as can be.

"That's the most fun I've had in ages, Carl. I can't wait to see what other romantic holiday ideas you've got up your sleeves."

"There's plenty more where that came from," I assure him. And I can't wait either. Thinking of how he faux-serenaded me on the ice, I have the perfect idea for our next fake date.

"Hey, so, this might not be super romantic, but our office usually gets together to go caroling to all the clients who sign up for it. And this is the first year since we started the tradition that Tina missed out. We stopped by her place, but that's not the same. What do you say I bring over my guitar and the three of us can have a night of caroling at her place?"

"Mom would love that. And so would I. It's a date."

Nick slings his arm around my shoulders and we resume walking through the warren of market booths. He walks me all the way to my car and kisses my cheek before we say goodnight. I drive home already eagerly counting down to the next time I get to see him.

Chapter 6

NICK—DECEMBER 19TH

MOM'S PLACE IS ALREADY neat as a pin, but I'm wandering around fluffing the couch cushions as I wait for Carl to come over. We've had to keep the floors spotless for Mom to get around with the walker the doctor wants her using while she recovers.

"Have you got ants in your pants, Nicholas? Sit and watch the movie." Mom gestures at me with her crochet hook. I can't sit still though. Everything has to look perfect and inviting for my date. The holiday romance on the screen can't hold my attention, but I sit obediently.

I have no illusions about myself. If Carl was the heroine of this movie, I'd be cast as the neglectful banker boyfriend from the big city. The villain everyone is supposed to root for her to dump in favor of the small-town Christmas tree farmer who sweeps her off her feet with holiday magic. Okay, the pronouns are confusing me with the analogy, but the point stands. If this was a movie, Carl would end up with someone like his ex, Saint.

I might not have it in me to be that attentive perfect boyfriend long-term, but I sure as heck can pretend for both our sakes. If it means sharing more mistletoe kisses and holding Carl's hand as we stroll past displays of twinkling lights, I'll pull out all the stops to make this week perfect. I want to drink down every drop of holiday cheer.

The doorbell rings, and I leap to my feet.

"I'll get it!" I call, dashing for the door like an anxious teenager with a crush.

"I know you will, dear." Mom cackles at me from her seat in the armchair amongst her crafting supplies.

She can somehow watch the Christmas movie without dropping a stitch on the tiny yarn outfits for more of her custom felted gnome tree ornaments. There's a pile of partially completed holiday crafts next to her on the coffee table. It's uncanny how she can turn scraps of yarn and the odds and ends from her bigger projects into art. Her customers seem to agree, judging from the non-stop business at her market stall.

I brush aside comparisons between how nice it is to interact with the public compared to the cold and calculating managerial work I do behind the scenes these days. Managing a team of creatives and fitting together all the pieces of the puzzle that go into getting their work in front of the right eyes is a far cry from the photography and digital design skills that got my foot in the door. It's a nice break to be in a customer facing role, however temporary it may be.

I take a moment to compose myself, running a hand through my hair and straightening out my warm flannel shirt before opening the door for Carl.

He's holding a guitar case in one hand and wearing the same bright blue parka from the night we met that brings out his gorgeous eyes. He grins and lifts the guitar. "Ready for some holiday music?"

"Can't wait," I nod and wave him inside. Carl stomps the snow from his boots before entering.

"Brr, think we might get some more snow before the big day." He shrugs out of his jacket and I take it to hang on a hook above the radiator so it will be warm when he has to leave later. "Thanks, Nick."

"No problem. Seems like we'll have a snowy Christmas, regardless. I can't remember the last time we had more than mucky sludge downtown." That isn't strictly true. My tiny balcony usually has a little patch of pristine snow, but it hardly counts. Not like the lovely blanket of untouched nature covering Mom's front yard.

"Mm, yeah, I remember that, how quickly the snow went from magical to a nuisance for the city to cart away as fast as possible when I lived there. It's one thing I like about moving back here."

"Shoveling the walkway? I'm not looking forward to that, but Mom needs a clear path with her walker, to get to her appointments and stuff."

"No, not shoveling. Snowball fights, obviously." He's grinning at me as he mimes packing and throwing a snowball, the mischief in his gaze leaves me with no doubt he still enjoys the childhood game. He's adorable.

"Snowball fights, huh?" I grab his scarf and tug him in for a chaste kiss.

Carl tenses at first. When I make no move to cop a feel or take it beyond the sweet movement of his lips on mine, he relaxes into the kiss. I keep a firm grip on his scarf to remind my hands not to wander. Carl licks into my mouth and his tongue tastes like Christmas, spicy gingerbread, molasses, and the crisp cool snow. I pull back to smile at him.

"Yeah, snowball fights. Wow. I didn't imagine it, huh?" Carl gazes into my eyes and I could get lost in him.

"Imagine what?" I lean in closer.

"That you're an exquisite kisser." Carl edges toward me.

"Mm? I wouldn't object to reminding you, if you forget again." I smile, inches from his face. Then I kiss the tip of his chilly nose and unwind his scarf to hang it next to his jacket.

"I promised Mom music, so we better not disappoint her. Come on, she's in the living room."

I turn to hide my erection and lead Carl down the hall. The thought of my mother waiting for us there is enough to quell my arousal. I might need to schedule time for some, uh, self-care before our next fake date, if this is how kissing him affects me. Taking it slow hasn't been an issue with my recent boyfriends, but I'm appreciating the space it gives us to get to know each other beyond the superficial.

With other guys, sex always starts out exciting until it becomes yet another area where I don't measure up to expectations. When I can only carve out so much time to be together, sex isn't always my first priority for what little time I have to spend with my partner. It's usually not worth the fighting to explain that I'd rather take care of that on my own. Especially if skipping sex means we have time for a nice dinner or to catch a show. It's a relief that Carl's rules about casual sex mean that won't be an issue for us.

Carl follows me down the hall. He goes right up to my mom to kiss her cheek. Oh, right; I almost forgot that they know each other. It didn't occur to me that he genuinely likes my mom. Weird. She almost never gets along with my boyfriends.

Mom hasn't said anything negative about my past boyfriends, she's just never this warm with them. Granted, I rarely bring them around and frequently can't find the time to keep dinner dates, let alone leave town to visit her, so that might be on me. I might need to work on that in the new year. Make time for the people in my life before I end up completely alone. That's a depressing thought, especially contrasted with the warm coziness of sitting in Mom's living room while she has a genuinely nice time with my—albeit fake—boyfriend.

"Hey, there Miss Tina, you're looking amazing! How are you feeling?" Carl smiles, giving her his full attention, like he really wants to know. I wish I had that kind of caring in my day-to-day life.

"Don't try to flatter me." Mom pats at her short perm self-consciously.

"I would never!" Carl clutches a hand to his chest in a 'who me?' gesture that brings a smile to my lips.

"I need to get my hair done, but Lucy says it won't take after the anesthesia, so I need to wait a few more weeks. Something to do with the chemicals." Mom waves away the information like it's an annoying fly. "Dr. Felleh seems happy with my physiotherapy progress and the pain is manageable at least."

"You listen to her, Dr. Felleh is one smart cookie." Carl wags his finger at Mom playfully, and she laughs, clearly not in the least intimidated by his teasing admonition.

It warms my heart to watch them interacting. Carl really is Mom's friend. She might not have been trying to set us up with all her hinting, but I'm certain she'd be thrilled if we dated for real. That gives me slight pause. But Mom doesn't have to know we're fake dating at all.

I'm only scheduled to be here for another two weeks, through the new year. This is just about having a fun holiday fling without all the messy entanglements, nothing serious.

"Bah, I'm fine, Carl. I'll be back in the office before you know it," Mom says airily. It will probably be a few more weeks to a month before that's true, but I admire her determination. Dr. Felleh says that's the biggest factor in recovery at her age. If so, she'll be fine.

"As long as you aren't overdoing it, we'll be happy to have you back." Carl nods.

"Speaking of cookies, where are my manners? Sit, make yourself at home. Nick, offer our guest refreshments."

"I'm fine, Tina, really," Carl protests.

"Here, sit," Mom makes to stand and clear several finished gnomes from the seat nearest her.

"I'll take care of that." He eases her back into her seat and steps in to stack the finished crafts neatly in a plastic tote before settling in on the couch. "No need to serve me, I'm here to be the entertainment."

"Nonsense. Nick, go get a plate of cookies. There should be some of the ones Beatrice left still in the kitchen." Half the town has stopped by with food and to check in on Mom, I swear. I'm not entirely sure which dishes came from each of the sweet elder women who have been by the house. But I know Mom's best friend, Beatrice, and I'm pretty sure she means the star-shaped sugar cookies decorated with enough icing to make a hockey fan cringe.

"Sure, of course. Coffee, Carl?" I'm reluctant to leave them, but Mom's right that I'm slacking at the hosting duties, just standing there like a lump while they chat.

"Sure, I take it with a splash of cream, if you don't mind? I'll just get this tuned while you take care of that." Carl hefts his guitar case onto his lap and unzips the fabric covering it.

"Oh, good. Here, I'll turn off the movie so you can hear better." Mom starts to get up again, but Carl and I both reach for the remote before she can stir from her chair.

Our fingers tangle on the buttons and there's a static spark as our eyes meet. His are full of mirth and I could lose myself in them. We both freeze and it's absurd, but that brief brush of our fingertips is more charged than a live wire. I don't want to stop touching him.

"Bah, I can turn off the TV without help!" Mom mutters something about overprotective young men and not being an invalid. I snort, because Carl went to high school at the same time as me, and almost forty hardly feels that young to me most days. I suppose on some level I'll always be the baby who surprised her later in life.

Carl chuckles, but he seems flustered as he averts his gaze and nudges the remote into my hand. Maybe I do feel a little young and reckless with a guy I like sitting in my mom's living room. I reluctantly pull away from his touch and power off the movie.

"I'll go make that coffee. Want anything Mom?"

"I'll have some of that nice gingerbread tea, dear. I'll be up half the night if I have coffee at this hour."

"Coming right up."

Carl strums a chord, and the thrum of music as he tunes his guitar follows me into the kitchen. I rush through the familiar tasks of making coffee and tea and piling one of Mom's decorative trays with several cookies for the three of us.

It's not long before he starts to play a song, "What Child is This." Mom sings along. I hum under my breath as I get out the cream and some honey for Mom's tea.

By the time I bring the tray of cookies and three full mugs into the living room, Mom and Carl have cleared a spot for our snacks. Most of her art supplies are back in their storage tote beside her chair. She still has her current project and a floppy ball of yarn in her lap.

Beside her, Carl is bent over his guitar. He seems to lose himself in the music as he transitions from the last few notes of one song and into the next. What would it be like to have time for hobbies? It's been ages since I actually took out my camera or did anything like skating for the sheer joy of it with Carl the other night. Without saying a word, Mom and Carl are making me realize how much I miss fun for its own sake.

The enraptured look on Carl's face as he plays almost makes me feel like I'm intruding on some sort of private communion with the music. Then he plucks out the tune for "Ding Dong Merrily on High." Our eyes meet, and it's like he's inviting me to come along as the music transports him.

Carl gives me an encouraging nod, like he's saying it doesn't have to be pitch-perfect as long as we're doing this together. He gives me permission to be messy and imperfect. I join in the next verse, slightly out of tune and letting it just be fun.

We sing until the barely touched coffee is cold and the cookies are nothing but crumbs. My voice feels raw, as if it might give out and I still don't want the night to end. Carl's rich tenor flows over me, warming me to my core. His hands on the guitar caress it as gently as a lover, coaxing beautiful music into the world. I wish I could freeze this moment. I always want to be caught in his smiling, joyful warmth.

As the final notes of "God Rest Ye Merry Gentlemen" fade, Mom stretches with a theatrical yawn.

"That was lovely, Carl. But on that note, I think it's time for me to rest these weary old bones."

"Good night, Miss Tina, I won't impose." He half-rises, reaching for his guitar case. I can't help the pang of loss. I'm not ready for this night to be over.

As if she's reading my mind, Mom waves Carl back to his seat. "Psh, you boys don't need to end your evening on my account. I'll be out like a light once I take my medications either way."

"Do you need any help, Mom?" I rise to bring her walker closer. She takes the assistance grudgingly.

"Can I help at all? I could put these little guys away? Or on your tree?" Carl holds up one of the gnome ornaments Mom finished while we sang. He glances around the living room with a growing furrow in his brow. "Where is your tree?"

"Oh, I didn't want to bother with one this year." Mom shrugs it off as though it's no big deal, but there's something off about her nonchalance.

She doesn't meet either of our gazes, pretending to organize yet another yarn project in the little basket of her walker. I know how much she adores decorating for the holidays, but it didn't occur to me to get her a tree because I rarely bother to decorate. That was boneheaded of me to assume she felt the same. Of course Mom wanted a tree.

"You know, with the surgery and all, I haven't had my usual energy to deal with decorating this year. And I've put too much on Nick's plate as it is."

She pauses to pinch my cheek affectionately as my stomach plunges. I believed her when she said she didn't want to go to the trouble of a tree this year. Now that she's laid it all out, I'm sick with shame at the realization she wanted one. She just didn't want to burden me with more work.

"It's no bother at all, Mom. I'll pick one up tomorrow."

"You don't have to do that, dear. It's a lot of work to keep it watered and tidy up after the needles that fall…"

"It only needs to last a few days at this point, Mom." I bend to kiss her cheek. "I can handle it. You barely need any help around here anymore, it will make me feel useful."

"Are you certain? It would be nice to have a tree up for the cookie swap on Friday." Mom glances wistfully to the spot in front of her broad bay windows where she usually places the tree.

"Consider it done," I promise.

Mom beams at me. "We'll need to get the ornaments from the attic."

"I'll handle that too, don't you try going up that rickety excuse for stairs without me."

"I can help," Carl offers. "My sister Gail's husband runs a farm that sells trees this time of year. I can get a great last-minute deal on the tree, delivery included."

"Thank you boys, I'm sure you can figure out the logistics without me." Mom beams at us both. "And now I really am off to bed. Thank you for a lovely evening, Carl."

"Good night, Miss Tina. It was a pleasure as always." Carl smiles.

"Don't be a stranger, dear." Mom winks at him, cutting her eyes meaningfully toward me, unable to resist a none-too-subtle nudge at matchmaking before making her way down the hall to her bedroom.

Carl watches her go, shaking his head with a bemused smile. "She sure is a force to be reckoned with."

"She is." I agree.

"Well, I should get going. We both have work in the morning." Carl reluctantly tucks his guitar back into its case and the zipper sounds too loud as it seals the end of our evening together. I'm not ready for this to be over. And apparently neither is Carl, because he lingers, sipping his cold coffee. "Shall we make the tree farm our next Christmas date?" he asks tentatively.

"I'd love to." I grin at him.

"Tomorrow on our lunch breaks?" Carl doesn't try to hide his enthusiasm and neither do I.

"It's a date."

Chapter 7

CARL—DECEMBER 20TH

I'M NOT SURE WHAT made me decide to bring Nick out to the farm to cut a tree for his mother ourselves. The market where I pick him up on my lunch break has perfectly good trees for sale, already cut and ready to transport. But the selection gets a little sparse so close to the holiday, and this is more fun.

Okay. I know why. It's romantic as all get out to do this together. I want to stroll through the winter wonderland of snow-laden branches, laughing and imagining each tree in a shared living room. I want to delight in that moment when the perfect tree catches both of our eyes and we talk over each other to declare, 'that's the one.' The one we'll be cuddled up next to on Christmas morning. Where we will tuck away gifts for each other with loving care.

I don't expect to indulge in the entire fantasy. It's not fair to expect Nick will want to sleep next to me when I made my no casual sex rule clear. It would be nice to wake up to someone in my bed on Christmas morning, but it's too big of an ask for a fake date. And we haven't really discussed exchanging gifts, so that's probably out too.

No, I can't live the elaborate fantasy spooling through my head on the short drive to the tree farm, but I can have tree shopping in the snow. A half hour spent picking something together to brighten the long winter nights.

My brother-in-law, Marcus, grins like the Cheshire cat when he sees me get out of Saint's SUV with Nick. He greets us and explains the process of how to find and cut our tree for Nick's benefit.

Marcus catches my eye to shoot me a thumbs up when Nick's back is turned. My sisters are going to know I'm seeing someone by the time we leave. Heck, knowing Marcus and Gail, half the town will know by nightfall. That's okay. Nick grew up here. He had to realize the entire town would gossip when he agreed to be my fake holiday fling. I'm just going to enjoy every magical moment while this lasts.

I twine our fingers and Nick takes that as a cue to lean in and kiss my cheek. Marcus looks like he's just dying to call Gail with the news. Oh well, let him. Nick is adorable as he talks animatedly about the perfect tree he has in mind. He doesn't release my hand as we turn toward the footpath Marcus points us toward.

We take the tarp, thick gloves, and bow saw that Marcus provides. Then we tromp along the worn snowy path past the rows and rows of young trees near the parking area. Those ones aren't quite large enough to cut yet. The tallest only comes up to chest height.

The snow is less trampled once we venture further into the trees. We reach the blue flags that mark the Fraser firs in the two meter height range and slow our pace to really examine each tree.

A flash of red catches my eye and a cardinal trills at us as it alights in the branches at the top of a gorgeous tree. The boughs are full, forming a gorgeous cone, and it's absolutely perfect.

"How about that one?" Nick asks.

"There!" I exclaim, laughing when I realize each of us is pointing at the same stunning tree where a second bright red cardinal lands next to the first and sidles in close. I'd love to take a page out of the birds' book, snuggling out in the snow.

"It's perfect!" I beam at him.

"Wonder if it comes with the cute little lovebirds." Nick grins back at me.

"Gay love birds." I point out. "Did you know the female birds are a dull brown color? So all the holiday greeting cards are gay or bi couples?"

"Mom mentioned that when she showed me her cardinal ornaments and explained why she made half of them brown."

"Oh, right! I forgot she was the one who told me that. She gave a pair of the brown ornaments to my sister Eliza and her wife as a wedding present ages ago."

"Cute."

"I think it's still their favorite ornament, but don't tell my niece that, since she's given them the obligatory handprint or photo ornaments every year since she was a toddler."

"My lips are sealed." Nick mimes zipping his lips. "Let's see about collecting this tree for Mom, eh?"

"Sure." I take the tarp from him and approach the tree, much to the cardinal couple's dismay. They whistle their displeasure as they take off in search of a better perch. I lay out the tarp so that the tree will hopefully land on it when we cut it down, crouching in the snow near the trunk to line it up.

"Do we just start cutting?" Nick circles the tree, grabbing one of the branches just as I lean in to figure out my angle to start cutting. The movement sways the tree enough to dislodge most of the snow, which falls on my shoulders with a heavy, wet splat. I gasp and arch away from the icy trickle down the back of my jacket.

"Oh!" I drop the saw near the trunk and jump to my feet to brush away the snow.

Nick bursts out laughing as I flail in place, trying to get the snow out of my shirt.

"It's cold!" I protest.

To his credit, Nick tries to wipe the smile off his face and appear sympathetic. He just can't quite pull it off even as he approaches to help me brush off the remaining snow.

I don't think before I scoop up a handful of snow and retaliate for his laughter by stuffing my fistful of powdery snow down his collar. It's Nick's turn to splutter and do the snow dance. He reaches up, grabs a tree branch and before I can fully form a protest, both of us are covered in snow.

"That's one way to clean off the branches," I guffaw.

"I think it was rather effective," he grins at me. "You cold?"

"Not yet. You do realize this means snow war, right?"

"Obviously."

We both squat down to scoop up snow, shaping it into ungainly projectiles. Nick ducks behind another tree for cover, laughing. We exchange a barrage of snowballs. Most of them land off target in harmless puffs of snow, but a few thud into each of our jackets. Nick gets one lucky shot that clips my ear.

I dart closer to get him back. The two of us chase each other in circles, throwing snow and acting like giddy teenagers until my fingers start to go numb and we're both breathless from laughter.

"How about a truce?" Nick calls across the churned snow between us.

"Not a chance!" I angle around to get a clearer line of sight to hurl my next snowball at him. It splats into the tree he's sheltering behind, which shakes and dumps more snow on his head.

"No fair!" he lobs a few more balls back at me in rapid succession. Then he breaks from cover to chase me with his hat stuffed full of snow.

"Last chance for a truce!" Nick offers when he tackles me into the snow, menacing me with the snow-filled hat.

"Not on your life!" I wriggle under him, the cold seeping into my pants.

"Remember, you asked for it." Nick shrugs.

Then he dumps his hatful of snow over my head and steals a quick kiss while I splutter in outrage.

"Okay, I surrender." I brush the snow from my face.

"Victory!" Nick fist pumps theatrically, which is a little awkward with him bracing himself over me one-handed now.

Nick grins as he kisses me once more, then rolls off of me, flopping onto his back beside me. We're both laughing and breathless, hands flung out between us so our fingers brush. Our breathing sounds harsh in the stillness, creating matching puffs of vapor.

I turn my head to examine his profile. Nick turns to face me. I can feel his body heat, foreheads nearly touching. We're so close. A hair's breadth from kissing in the snow.

"Thank you, Carl. I haven't laughed that much in ages."

Well, short of pressing our cold lips together to warm us up, I can't think of a response to that. So I give in to the impulse to kiss him. He moans into my mouth, but he doesn't try to roll back on top of me or make the sweet moment into something it isn't.

Nick cups my cheek in his hand, fingers combing through my beard. We stay there kissing until the damp chill of the snow gets to be too much. We still have to finish getting our tree before we head back to the real world.

"Shit, I'm going to be late reopening the booth." Nick curses when he notices the time.

We both get up and I indulge in brushing loose snow off his ass for him. Nick grins at me. Hopefully, the cold is enough to keep him from being too disappointed that this isn't going any further than making out in the snow.

It's a thrill to touch him with impunity. I'm used to dates pushing for more if I give an inch. In contrast, Nick has been nothing but respectful of my boundaries. It's a welcome change from the sort of expectations I've encountered from most of my past dating attempts. I'm trying to ignore the fact that all this romantic sweetness comes with an expiry and just enjoy the time we have together, but it's hard not to wish this was real.

"Me too. Let's grab the tree and Marcus will have it delivered to your mom's place tonight."

"Are you getting me special treatment? He can't possibly offer same-day delivery for every tree?"

"Friends and family deal. It's fine." I finish shaking the last remnants of snow from our tree to make transporting it easier. Nick helps me to shake the snow off the tarp and arrange it next to the tree again. We make an efficient team, lining it up for the tree to land on once more. "He's already bringing one into town tonight for Eliza's party. Your mom's place isn't far out of his way."

"You're sure?" Nick bites his lip adorably.

"Positive." I hip check him playfully and he gives me a return shove.

I pull on the thick gloves Marcus gave us to protect my hands in case the saw slips. Then I set its teeth against the bark at the base of the trunk. Even with the manual blade, it's only the work of a moment to cut through the narrow trunk. We work together to guide the tree down to the tarp to haul back to the parking lot.

"Fine, you can have it delivered later," Nick concedes, then he flashes me a hopeful smile. "But you aren't getting out of helping us trim the tree that easily; come over tonight?"

"Yeah, I'd, uh, like that. A lot." I stare at him a little too long, wondering if this man can read my mind. Or if he shares the same romantic notions that I have about the perfect holiday season with my dream date. It's just my luck that the perfect guy exists, but I can only have him for a week. No sense dwelling on that. "Come on. We should get back."

I take the excuse to twine our fingers again, and we walk back to the car, close enough that our shoulders bump with every other step. It's getting harder and harder to remember this isn't real, but damn, Nick is good at making all my romantic imaginings come true. Like my own personal Saint Nick, granting every Christmas wish I've ever made.

Chapter 8

CARL—DECEMBER 20TH

Even though I made plans with Nick, I have a weird moment of expecting Tina to be the one to greet me at her front door when I arrive. I've been here a few times in the past for team building dinners, fiber crafting nights, and the occasional visit. Last night, it was a relief to see Tina just as vivacious as ever only a few weeks out from her surgery.

Too many of our clients at Days of Grace, my nonprofit eldercare and drop-in center, have gotten similar procedures and came out the other side seeming frailer for it. I'm glad Tina seems to be recovering well. And even gladder when her son opens the door and takes my breath away with his gorgeous smile.

I'm freshly showered, having come straight here from my standing gym date with Saint. The sight of Nick standing in Tina's door still hits me with the urge to check that I don't have armpit stank. It's absurd how much I like this guy already.

Nick opens his arms for a hug that I walk right into. His arms around me are pure comfort. I tip my face up toward him for a kiss and he gives it, soft and sweet, hands rubbing my arms before we step apart.

"Hey, babe. Glad to see me?" I ask.

"Always. You've got impeccable timing. I just finished wrestling our beast of a tree into the stand. I didn't realize it would be so much work to get it level, or I might have waited for you."

"Ah, you should have! I'd have helped with that. Saint held mine up while I adjusted it for my tree," I admit. Then I flush with the familiar rising tide of anxiety at mentioning my best friend to a date. People get weird about how close we still are. Especially once they know about our relationship history.

"Next time I will." Nick grins at me. I guess he doesn't mind—which makes sense with him leaving in a week. "Mom's friends came to take her for a coffee so we can surprise her with the finished tree. I swear the darn thing looks three times bigger now that it's inside."

"Not too big, I hope?" I chuckle as I follow him into the living room. "Things always seem bigger once you get them inside." I choke on the last word when Nick glances back at me and winks.

I have to play the phrase back to realize why he's making that knowing face. Oh. Right. Does he think I'm making a veiled comment about his dick feeling bigger in my ass?

Do I want that with him? Eh. Would I consider it if that was the only way to keep being the focus of his dazzling smile and sweet kisses?

Maaaybe? I should have learned my lesson about those sorts of compromises by now, but—well, the heart wants what it wants. And sometimes sex is nice. Not all the time, but I could see it being fun with Nick, considering how much heart he's put into everything else we've done together so far. If he could be content with my low sex drive, I could see it being nice.

The temptation to ignore my boundaries won't be an issue with Nick, because this is temporary. Tonight is more of the lovely wish fulfillment we agreed to. Trimming the tree with a boyfriend—check.

Christmas carols are playing from a speaker on Tina's mantel, a cozy fire is blazing on the hearth, albeit one of those decorative propane ones with fake logs. Nick has coils and coils of Christmas lights and overflowing boxes of ornaments spread across every surface of Tina's living room, like a holiday store exploded in here.

The decorations are all totally Tina's style, kitschy and cute, perfect for a cozy family holiday celebration. And the tree is even more quintessentially perfect, standing here in the warm living room with a gorgeous man smiling as he invites me to help him deck his halls.

"These are all good to go." Nick picks up a strand of glowing lights and unplugs it to check whether the next coil works. He must have been testing the strands when I arrived. He brings the first coil over to the ladder next to the tree and starts winding the lights around the tree from the top down. "That's the last of them, so it looks like we've got plenty to work with."

"Excellent." I rub my hands together. "Let's light her up!"

"Sure, take this?" Nick holds out the coil of lights when he gets to the edges of his reach.

"Sure. This is going to look fantastic." I pass it around the tree and back to him. As we work at spooling the lights down the tree, I peruse the ornaments. I go to get another strand each time we run out of length. Before long, we get to the lowest branches and Nick plugs in the end of the last strand.

"Wow!" Joy bubbles up in my chest at the warm golden glow of the lights. "It's perfect."

Nick loops his arm around my waist and rests his head on my shoulder to admire our handiwork at my side. "It's getting there. Next is draping mom's rustic garland on the tree, the window sills, and the mantle."

I follow his directions to transform the living room into Tina's perfect woodland Christmas fantasy-scape. Felted gnomes and woodland creatures peek out from behind glittering pinecone and felted mushroom garlands. The tree matches in muted earth tones.

We're running low on the last box of tree ornaments when "Rockin' around the Christmas Tree" streams from the speakers. I can't help dancing my way around the tree as I place the final fox peeking out of the soft fir needles. I dance, utterly unselfconscious until I notice Nick watching me like I'm the most interesting sight in the room. He licks his lips, like he wants to say something but can't find the words.

"Dance with me?" I offer him my hand. Nick hesitates before taking it and letting me twirl him into the dance. We rock around the tree, then bop along to the next singer, belting out that all she wants for Christmas is you. Just like at the skating rink, the song reaches inside and squeezes my heart. And when the song changes to slower crooning, Nick lets me pull him into a close hold so we can sway together.

Nick gazes into my eyes like they hold all the secrets of the universe and I don't shy away, because what if they do? Nick follows my lead as effortlessly as if we've been dancing together for years.

Is this what it's like to be swept off my feet? It's nothing like falling in love has been for me in the past. No breathless loss of gravity as I brace for the landing, just moving from joy to joy and giving myself to all of it, no holding back.

This is the sort of attentive love I'm going to hold out for when Nick goes back to the city: someone who meets me where I am. Who hears my wistful stories of snowball fights and gives me one. Who is willing to follow where I lead. Breathless kisses, sweet touches, no demands.

We sway in place as the last lines of the song fade. I'm caught in his gravity, our bodies melded together from chest to groin. Our lip merge as if we're magnetized. I can't stop kissing Nick. I hold his hips snug to my body and his hands caress the sides of my neck and along my jaw, deepening the kiss.

"Wow, this place looks fantas—Oh, goodness!" Tina's voice wrenches me a step back from her son as she bursts into startled laughter. She has one hand on her walker and the other pressed to her chest as she smiles at us. "Here I was thinking we were past the phase where I had to worry about walking in on you with a boy, Nick!"

"Sorry, Mom." Nick gives her a rueful smile as he scratches at the back of his head. "We finished decorating and, uh, got a little carried away."

"You're both grown men." Tina waves away his apologetic explanation. "Feel free to get as carried away as you'd like; just consider doing it in your bedroom before any clothes come off?"

"Mom!"

"Miss Tina, I'm not that kind of boy!" I protest in my campiest tone. But I can't quite dredge up any real heat to my feigned outrage through the roiling in my gut at all the assumptions rife in their gentle banter. Like, of course, the next step here is getting naked and fucking. As if this golden and glittering moment isn't enough all on its own. As if I'm not enough. I swallow back the lump of raw emotion in my throat.

"I should get going." I edge away from Nick.

His fingers trail down from my shoulder and over the back of my hand. Instead of letting my fingers drop from his grip, he squeezes my hand, wordlessly asking me to stay.

I can't face this right now though.

"What? No, dear! I'm sorry if I embarrassed you. Of course, you can stay as late as you want." Tina looks mortified at the thought she might have shamed me into leaving.

"No, it's fine. Just late. We have so much to do at work before the holidays, and I've got an early bird drop-in Santa's breakfast group tomorrow."

"Oh, I might see you there. For the cookies, you understand."

"Your doctor hasn't cleared you for work yet." I plant my hand on my hip, my equilibrium restored as we move to firmer conversational ground.

"Psh. I'll come as a visitor then. The cookies compel me." Tina winks.

"Of course, just for the cookies." I snort with laughter. "I can't stop you, as long as you're up for it."

"Oh, speaking of cookies, the ladies saw your car out front and wanted me to invite you to our annual swap on Friday. I know it's short notice, but I wasn't sure I'd be up for hosting sooner."

"Are you kidding? I wouldn't miss your cookie swap. How many cookies do I need to bring?"

"Six dozen? There are around ten guests coming, so that will be enough of each type for everyone to take at least half a dozen."

"Sure." I dart a glance toward Nick, bite my lip and commit. This is still happening. We are still pretending our way to the perfect holiday week. Where I can be everything he wants and have all my dreams come true. "Nick, would you want to come over tomorrow night and help me bake them?"

"Sure! I'll be there with silver bells on." He smiles so sweetly at me. I lean in to kiss his dimpled cheek, then I hug Tina and take my leave with one last backward glance at Nick.

Chapter 9

NICK—DECEMBER 21ST

I FIND PARKING ACROSS the street from Carl's adorable townhouse. The entire building is dripping in bright icicle lights, like a frosted gingerbread house. Carl's side of the duplex also has a single LED candle lit in each window and a wreath on the door.

The tree in the front window glows in a riot of rainbow lights and colorful ornaments. I drink in the sight of it with a smile on my face. His home is bursting with all the holiday cheer that so encapsulates the man I'm falling for—whoa, am I falling for Carl?

I take a moment in the car to compose myself, hands clenched on the steering wheel. I'm nervous to see Carl again after how fast he bolted last night. It was obvious he wasn't comfortable with how we left things.

I hope his hasty retreat wasn't because I was hard enough to pound nails when Mom walked in on us. This might not be a real relationship, but it may still be time to have a more in-depth conversation about how sex fits into things between us.

Temporary or not, things with Carl don't feel casual anymore. They don't feel fake either, but my track record with relationships is abysmal. I can't see that improving with long-distance thrown into the equation once Mom is well enough for me to return to my life in the city.

I should keep my mouth shut and enjoy the good times while they last. Follow Carl's lead when it comes to the kisses that are turning me inside out and leaving me wanting so much more of him.

Which means I need to go inside and face whatever uncomfortable conversation we need to have about last night. And then we can still hopefully make cookies as planned. Carl mentioned gingerbread while we were texting and I want nothing more than to taste his holiday spiced lips.

I get out of the car, pocketing my keys. As I mount the steps up to Carl's place, the door on the other side of the duplex opens. A burst of throaty laughter precedes a stranger with striking features and long dark hair.

"Call me?" The stranger holds their hand up to their face, their thumb and pinkie extended in a gesture to match the request. Saint, standing in the entryway in nothing but a taupe bathrobe, loops a scarf around the back of his guest's neck. He uses the ends to draw them close for a lingering kiss.

"Bye, Angel." Saint releases his grip on the scarf and gives his hookup a nudge out the door.

"Bye, Saint. I'll see you around." Angel—I wonder if that's a pet name—sighs.

They have a sad little smile fixed in place as they turn toward the sidewalk. They tuck their scarf around their neck against the winter chill. It's clear they didn't miss Saint dodging the promise, and equally clear that they're smitten with Carl's handsome ex. More luck to them.

"So, you're the reason Carl has been swooning around on cloud nine all week?" Saint catches my eye and leans laconically on his door jamb. His eyes track Angel down the snowy sidewalk as he addresses me. It's possible Angel's continued interest isn't as one-sided as Saint's stoic facade made it seem—not my business. Then again, my relationship with Carl isn't Saint's business either. Not beyond whatever details Carl wants to share with him.

"We've been on a few dates," I admit. Vain hope bubbles up in my chest. Carl genuinely seems to like me. It's still oddly thrilling to hear that from an outside perspective, as if his outward happiness being remarked upon by his friends makes it more real. Not that I can do anything about my growing feelings. I push aside the glum thought and focus on our plan for a perfect holiday season.

"Good. Carl has a lot of love to give the right guy," Saint says, arms crossed over his chest. Defensive? Or he could just be cold standing there in a bathrobe. "And he likes you, so don't screw it up."

"Like you did?" The words escape before I can bite them back. Some macho-grandstanding, insecure part of me that wants to challenge his place in Carl's life is glad I said it. Heeding my more mature impulses, I rush to utter an apology. "Sorry, that was uncalled fo—"

"That's not quite how things went down." To my surprise, Saint chuckles. He tears his eyes off the corner where Angel turned out of sight to meet my eyes. There's a hint of a smile in his twinkling eyes even as he tries to look serious. "Neither of us screwed up; we just make better friends than lovers, and I'll leave it to him to explain the details of that if and when he's ready to share. But when he does, be kind to him or you and I will have a problem."

"I will keep that in mind." It's an easy promise to make; I can't see myself being unkind to Carl, no matter what details of their relationship Saint is alluding to. It would be like kicking a puppy.

"Good man." Saint straightens up and reaches to clap me on the shoulder. "Well? Don't keep him waiting, he's excited. Bestie kept me up half of last night talking my ear off about which cookies were the most romantic." Saint rolls his eyes, but he's grinning as he mutters something that sounds like 'alimony' under his breath. Then he goes back into his side of the duplex, leaving me to knock on Carl's door. Carl mentioned that being a running joke between them.

Saint must have been right that Carl is excited. He opens the door as I'm midway through knocking.

"Hey! Did you find the place alright?" Carl steps aside. "Come on in and make yourself at home. It's freezing out there. Brr." He shivers theatrically and I can't help grinning at him.

"Hi." I want to pull him into my arms and kiss him in greeting, but I'm not sure where we stand on kisses after how last night ended. Instead, I stomp the snow off my boots. Then I step inside and shut the door before removing my outerwear. "I'm sure the baking will have me nice and toasty soon enough."

"It will." Carl grabs my jacket and hangs it in his hall closet while I line my boots up next to his in front of his baseboard heater. "I arranged all the ingredients, so we can get started right away, if you want?"

"I want." Fuck it, this is our week of wish fulfillment and I want to kiss my holidate every chance I get. "But first, I really want to kiss you again. Is that alright?"

"Oh. Yes. Please." Carl's eyes flutter shut as I lean in to tip up his chin and press our lips together. He sighs out a happy little noise against me. It's unreal that I've only been kissing him for a few days when we meld together so perfectly. I pull back and try to memorize his face and this moment.

"Mm." I thumb over his full lips as I gaze into his eyes. "That is never going to get old."

"Yeah," Carl agrees breathily.

"I wasn't sure if you wanted to stop after last night."

"No! I don't want to stop. I just... don't want to, uh, keep going past that?" Carl fidgets, not quite meeting my gaze.

"I got that impression. Because this still seems casual to you or...?" I shrug, unsure how to finish the sentence.

Carl turns to fiddle with a gorgeous poinsettia sitting on a stand by the door. "It's not that I don't like what we're doing. But it's not real, right? It's going to end when you go back to Toronto and that's going to be hard enough without complicating things for no reason."

Adding orgasms with someone I can't get out of my head to our storybook holiday fling hardly seems like no reason. Something about Saint's not-quite-shovel-talk makes me think that there's more to this. And that Carl has probably had bad reactions in the past. I can take a no.

"Okay. Whatever you're comfortable with. I won't push for more than kissing."

"You're sure that's enough?"

"More than enough. This is the best December I can remember. So. Ready to make sweet, sweet cookies?" I try to lighten the mood, waggling my eyebrows.

Carl laughs as he leads me to his kitchen.

He really does have all the ingredients out. Instrumental holiday music is playing softly from a speaker. His house is tastefully decorated for the season wherever I look. Holiday cards hang from neat rows of festive string twisted to look like candy canes. The cards are clipped evenly along their lengths, covering one wall of his hallway. Dozens of cards. Even if most of them are from acquaintances or work connections, that's far more people than I can even wrap my head around adding to my personal holiday card list.

Is that really any wonder with how friendly he is? No, but it strikes me that his life is full of friends and family and mine is... well, as pristinely barren and empty as my apartment back in the city.

These past few weeks helping Mom with her craft booth and now getting to know Carl are the happiest I've had in years. I'm not going to do anything to upset our arrangement prematurely. So I let any deeper conversation fall by the wayside. I roll up my sleeves and set to making another holiday memory.

Carl reads out the measurements and I hand him what he needs. We laugh more than anyone ought to when I turn on the mixer too fast to incorporate the dry ingredients and the powder flies everywhere. When we roll out the dough, I feel like a kid again at the selection of cookie cutters he has for us to choose from. We make an army of gingerbread people, a forest of Christmas trees, and a galaxy of cookie stars. Along with a herd of assorted dinosaurs for good measure.

Carl's house smells amazing as the last batch comes out of the oven and we carefully transfer the cookies to wire racks to cool. Carl regales me with stories about holidays past. We both laugh at the one time when Saint tried to make him a batch of cookies to cheer him up after a bad day. He confused the cocoa powder with instant espresso. Carl tells it with the pleasant nostalgia of a well-worn memory.

I don't think anyone aside from my mother has ever told that sort of fond tale about me. Where you can hear how much the teller loves the subject in every syllable. It doesn't precisely make me jealous of his bond with Saint, but I envy their closeness.

"So, the cookies came out awful, but of course I ate them anyway. Saint isn't really one for grand gestures, but he knows I am, so he tried." Carl finishes the story with a chuckle as he starts mixing the icing for the cookies. "Anyway, they were bitter as sin, and packed enough of a caffeine punch to keep us both up all night."

"I'd have figured you wouldn't need cookies for that." I laugh at the anecdote.

Instead of laughing at my joke, the mirth leaves Carl's face. He presses his lips into a tight line.

"That was post marriage. The only all nighters Saint was pulling those days were to study for his bar exam."

"Oh." Shit, that was a boneheaded thing for me to say. Obviously, his emotions about their previous relationship are complicated. I have so many questions about how they managed to stay so close after such a huge upheaval, but they're too personal. Asking will only bring the mood down further when we're supposed to be enjoying an evening of wholesome holiday baking. "Sorry."

I don't know what to say to bring back the sparkle in Carl's eye. So I reach toward him, resting my hand palm up next to the mixer. Carl grabs it and squeezes, and it feels like absolution. He goes back to measuring out all the powdered sugar for the icing.

A puff of sugar rises from the bowl when Carl turns on the mixer. Carl yelps and slaps at the slider to slow down the paddle. He wipes the back of his hand over his face, leaving a smudge on the tip of his nose.

"Phew, that was almost a disaster." Carl favors me with a lopsided grin.

I'm struck by the urge to kiss away the sugar on his skin. It might come close to being as sweet as he is. I tear my gaze from his face to the icing. There's so much of it whirling around the bowl, but we'll need it to decorate our entire assortment of gingerbread creations.

As a kid, Mom's cookie swaps with her friends were a highlight of my holiday season. Right up there with Santa. It always seemed like magic when the trays of familiar sugar cookies Mom made had multiplied into dozens of different recipes overnight. Melt in your mouth rum balls, jewel-toned jam cookies, spritz cookies decorated like tiny wreaths, white chocolate dipped gingersnaps, and the list went on. Every festive flavor and shape imaginable spread out in a cookie breakfast buffet the morning after the party.

"Almost done. Want to grab the box of baggies by the microwave and we can mix up the colors?" Carl pulls me out of my memories of cookies past. He still looks adorable with a dusting of powdered sugar in his beard and that smudge on his nose. Fuck it.

I lean in to kiss his nose, cupping his face in my hand. He smiles sweetly at me.

"Sure. I'll get right on that," I say, fingers lingering on his chin.

Carl pulls me in for a proper kiss and I want to melt into his arms and forget everything but his lips on mine. I could live in the gentle caress of his tongue against mine, contrasting with the warm scrape of his bushy beard on my cheeks. His arms squeeze around me, the solid planes of his back are firm under my hands. Too bad we don't have time to get distracted from the dozens of cookies we need to decorate for tomorrow.

"We should finish the cookies," Carl breaks off the kiss, echoing my thoughts.

"Right." I lick my lips, wishing I could keep tasting him instead.

We get back to our delicious work, snacking on spare cookies and comparing favorite holiday memories as we go, until I'm giddy from the sugar and spending time with Carl. The trays of completed cookies soon outnumber the ones still left to do.

"Did you ever go to the tree decorating party in Nathan Phillips Square?" Carl asks as he adds bright red spots to a T-Rex cookie. "The Cavalcade of Lights was one of my favorite parts of the season when we lived in Toronto."

"Can't say that I have. I'm sure it's a great event, but I never seem to find time for things like that back home, unless it's to woo a client."

"Well, it's awesome. You should make the time next year. They light up the big tree, there's a DJ, live music, skating, dancing, and circus performers. And they top off the night with fireworks. It's the perfect kickoff to the holiday season. And there's all the little holiday markets all over."

"I'm sure Toronto has nothing on the Elk's Pass Holiday market." There's a kernel of truth to my gentle teasing. The night I met Carl there will forever live in my memories as one of the most romantic dates of my life, fake or otherwise.

"Sure. We have a lovely tree lighting party here too. And the skating rink has been popular since they added it a few years back. I'm guessing you haven't been to the light parade either, then?"

"Not since I was a kid. Isn't that this week?" I have vague memories of floats with people in winter-themed costumes throwing tiny candy canes into the crowd and a jolly Santa Claus waving at the end.

"Tomorrow." Carl nods.

"We should go!" I say.

Carl bites his lip. "It's at the same time as your mom's cookie swap."

"Oh. Well, can we figure out a way to do both? Drop off the cookies, go to the parade and then back to the swap? I'll ask Mom what she thinks. If it weren't for her surgery making scheduling complicated, you know she'd never double-book something like that."

"Sure." Carl grins at me. "I'm just glad she's recovering so quickly, your mom is one tough cookie."

"You are not allowed to pun about my mom," I scold him to hide my chuckle.

"Fine, I won't mention that having to choose one event is just how the cookie crumbles." Carl winks at me, eyes bright with the same mirth I feel in his presence. "Oh, right, speaking of parties, do you have a Christmas sweater for Eliza's party on Saturday? It's sort of a thing. We vote on the best and worst sweaters."

"No, but I'm sure I can find something at the market tomorrow on one of my breaks."

"Nice. I can help you look during my lunch break?"

"Yeah, I'd love that." I can't seem to stop smiling around Carl.

The more time I spend with him, the less I want this to end and to have to return to the real world and all my responsibilities. But Mom is getting back on her feet and there's only so much time I can justify taking off now that she's getting around better on her own. We've got things set up so she won't have to do any heavy lifting once I get the holiday crafts put away after the market closes on Christmas Eve.

This perfect bubble of happiness is doomed to end soon, but until it does, I'm going to enjoy every moment with Carl. I reach for the blue icing to put snowflakes on the white background that I already frosted on several star cookies. At the same time, Carl goes to give his latest dinosaur blue splotches. My fingers tingle where our hands brush.

I revel in the way the tension between us coils low in my gut. Thousands of fantasies of twining our fingers, then sweeping aside the cookies to make passionate love to him unspool in my head. I ignore them all.

I withdraw my hand to let Carl have the blue icing. These cookies can have some red holly berries instead. Carl stares intently at his dinosaur, cheeks flushed, and I know he felt that same spark. I want him more than I've wanted anyone in ages, but I'm going to follow his lead. Better to bank the flames of my longing than to let them consume what time we have left of our deal. I won't ask for something Carl isn't ready to share with me.

This time spent with him is more than enough. His laughter and smiles as he playfully arranges his completed dinosaurs under my array of painted stars is better than any orgasm. Each story and joke he shares with me is better than a wordless moan, or my name on another lover's lips. His fingers brushing mine as we exchange colorful bags of icing are better than the most intimate touches from my exes. In short, he's everything I want and more, and I wouldn't trade one second together for anything.

Chapter 10

CARL—DECEMBER 22ND

I PICK NICK UP from the market with our carefully packaged cookies already loaded into the back seat. With only a few days remaining before it closes, the market is a bustling hive of activity, even as most of the vendors are closing up for the night.

As we leave, folks have already started to line up along the parade route, staking out the best spots, and Main Street is blocked to traffic. We have to take a circuitous route along residential streets to avoid the parade's path.

We park a few blocks away and have to dash across Main to get to Tina's place at the end of a cul-de-sac. If both our hands weren't full carrying our dozens of cookies, I'd twine my fingers with Nick's. We make our break for it to cross the snowy pavement, laughing and smiling in the crisp cold of the evening. Volunteers with the parade wave us urgently off the road. We have to weave through a wall of folding chairs and dodge parents pulling little kids in sleds on the sidewalk.

We take the turn into Tina's quiet tree-lined neighborhood, where all the houses are lit and each garish outdoor display vies to outdo its neighbors. Nick must have been the one to drag the two lit-up mesh reindeer onto his mother's front lawn. They're understated compared to the dozens of inflatable decorations her neighbors have running. A giant Frosty the snowman waves next to a snow globe with cartoon characters in holiday garb inside.

The neighborhood sports several Santas in various postures, including cartoon characters dressed as him or his elves. One house boasts blinking blue and white lights and a glowing menorah next to a giant inflatable polar bear holding a dreidel. Across the street, a family of inflatable gnomes stands next to a house with a snowman wearing a red, black, and green scarf. Whoever lives there covered the windows behind the snowman in Kwanzaa themed window clings.

Everywhere I look, there are decorations and signs of holiday cheer. It's a chaotic celebration of the season that has me grinning from ear to ear next to Nick as we take in all the bright lights.

When we reach Tina's door, the party is already in full swing. Beatrice, one of Tina's closest friends who sometimes volunteers at Days of Grace, greets us at the door. She welcomes us in with kisses on the cheeks and exclamations about how good our cookies look. We follow Beatrice through the living room, where Tina sits ensconced in her favorite arm-chair, chatting with several of her guests.

"Carl, Nick! You're the last ones to arrive, so we can get started!" Tina exclaims. She levers herself up with her walker and pulls me into a hug made awkward by my armful of cookies.

She hugs her son next, then shoos us all into the kitchen, not letting her surgery slow her down in the least. Even if she does have to lean heavily on the walker as she shepherds us all along to the main event of the evening.

I follow Beatrice into the kitchen. Every surface is covered in tins, trays, and tupperwares overflowing with a vast array of cookies. Tina hands out decorative tins for each guess to collect our half dozen cookies from each of the varieties on offer. We're soon swallowed into a crowd of the ladies and the handful of gents who I work with. We all circulate around the displays of cookies, taking some of each to fill our boxes.

Nick and I are soon separated, and part of me worries he'll be out of his depth. How many times have dates commented that my closeness with the elderly folks I work with is weird? I can't help the gnawing worry that a gathering like this being my idea of a good time might be a huge turn off for Nick. But every time I catch a glimpse of him, he's deep in conversation with his mom's friends. And every time our eyes catch, he dazzles me with his smiles. Like he's enjoying this as much as I am.

It's almost worse to know he could be happy fitting into my typical not-so-wild Friday nights like this. That he could be content to join me catching up on gossip, nibbling cookies, and comparing notes on the various crafting projects Tina's guests are working on.

Most of the time when we all get together, at least half of the guests have fiber art projects with them. Tonight isn't much different. Once the cookies are distributed and packed up to go home with each guest, most of the party migrates to the living room.

Tina has Nick put on decaf coffee and tea for everyone. She delegates setting the coffee table with more pastries and fruit and veggie trays for the crowd to nibble on. Beatrice badgers her back to her seat where she presides over a crafting night in the living room with holiday music playing softly in the background.

"Be a dear and help me grab my knitting bag, Carl?" Beatrice loops her elbow through mine, and I know this is completely a ploy to have my ear. Beatrice is far from frail, even in her late seventies.

"Of course, Miss Bea. How have you been?" I walk across the living room with her to get her knitting bag from the entryway closet.

"Tina tells me you boys set up the tree for her the other night; it looks lovely, Carl." Beatrice beams as she grabs the bag from the hook in the closet.

"Thanks." I smile as I watch Nick delivering warm beverages to his mom's other guests.

"She also tells me you've been spending most of the week with her son." She looks meaningfully between me and Nick. "Anything there?"

I try to hide my flush by turning to track Nick's progress across the room. He looks so right in my life. I wish this could be more than a fake fling. I wish love could fit this seamlessly into my life, but after all the ways I don't fit, I'm not sure I'll ever have anything this good for real. "It's too soon to say, and he's going back to Toronto next month."

"Hm. Are you certain of that?"

"Yes."

"Ah, Tina must have been mistaken about how miserable he's been in the city then. She says this is the happiest she's seen Nick in years."

"Has he said anything to her about staying in Elk's Pass?"

"No. But she's been thinking of downsizing. My neighbor at Caribou Heights is moving in with her son in Vaughn, and Tina seems interested in the neighborhood. I know she plans to offer Nick a good price on the house before she lists it."

"Oh." Hope flares in my chest that this could become a lasting love. "It's only been a few days, though."

"Don't be too hasty to write off love, Carl. I told Tina that I was going to marry my Robert the first night we met, you just ask her if I didn't! And that man and I shared fifty wonderful years together before he passed. Sometimes the heart knows what the head is too thick to accept."

"I'll, uh, keep that in mind." I take the bag from Beatrice and let her lead me back into the living room.

If Beatrice is right, and if Nick takes his mom up on the offer... I ruthlessly crush back the thousands of happy what-ifs that explode in my chest. My longing for that beautiful future is an almost physical ache. What if I could let myself fall for Nick for real? Too many ifs to hang my heart on.

He only promised me our one perfect holiday week, and he hasn't said a thing about wanting more than that. It's easy to overlook my closeness with my ex and the lack of sex and all my other foibles for a week. How many times have I seen those things turn from lovable quirks into deal breakers over the years? No. I can't have Nick forever. But I can enjoy this while it lasts.

I heft Beatrice's bag over to the sofa for her. She claims her seat on the couch nearest to Tina's chair. Tina presides over the gathering to ensure everyone feels welcome in her home, ever the gracious host.

"Carl, my son tells me that you boys wanted to watch the parade." Tina cuts her eyes to the clock over the mantle. "If you go now, you should be able to catch most of it. This is usually around the time the first few floats reach Elm Crescent."

"Are you sure?"

"Psh, go. Just because these old bones are too finicky to enjoy standing in the cold for an hour doesn't mean you shouldn't indulge. You can both come back and warm up with a coffee afterward." Tina waves us toward the door.

"Or Nick can enjoy his coffee back at your place. I'm sure Tina will hold on to your cookies until morning for you," Beatrice interjects. Her knitting needles continue clacking away as she gives me a wink all the while continuing to add even rows of stitches. The woman is a menace.

"Bea!" Nick protests.

"We're taking it slow, you dirty old woman," I tease her.

Beatrice scoffs. "Go have a good time so we can live vicariously through you."

"What do you think?" I ask.

"Let's do it." Nick reaches for my hand and the two of us hurriedly don our outerwear and venture back into the cold, hand in hand.

"I hope what Beatrice said didn't make you uncomfortable." I venture as we approach the end of the street.

Nick smiles at me. "Nah, I'm used to her lack of filter by now. She and Mom have been thick as thieves practically forever."

"Yeah. She's irrepressible."

"Oh, I can hear the music. Come on, we should hurry so we don't miss it!" Nick grabs my hand and pulls me into the crowd on the sidewalk to admire the lights and music. The part of me that hasn't given up on the perfect holiday romance is giddy as he grins back at me. He seems as eager as I am to drink in every drop of holiday magic.

Nick doesn't release my hand when we find a vantage next to a family with several laughing children. They're adorable, making grabby hands at the elves on foot next to the high school marching band handing out candy.

I stand pressed up against my date as the parade marches past. A perfect holiday dusting of snow drifts down on us like sifted sugar melting on our tongues. It's hard to live in this moment when Beatrice dangled the possibility of having him for more than a few dates in front of my face. I try my damnedest not to miss out on the moments I do have with Nick by yearning too hard for what I can't have.

Chapter 11

NICK—DECEMBER 22ND

"So, you could come back to my place for coffee. If you want?" Carl won't meet my eyes as we watch the crowd disperse into the night. The last few flashing lights behind the Santa float pass out of sight around a bend in the road. I get the impression he's no more ready for the night to end than I am.

"Sure." I nod. "I can bring your cookies to you tomorrow before your sister's party, so we don't have to face Beatrice's teasing."

"She means well, but yes, I'd just as soon avoid that. Just, um, one thing?" Carl licks his lips, drawing my attention to just how much I want to kiss him here in the snow.

"Sure, what's up?" It's on the tip of my tongue to offer him anything he wants, or voice a flippant flirtation about how coffee never means coffee. Even though I've wished that wasn't true countless times before. When a date goes well and I want to keep the conversation flowing all night long, but it somehow always flows right into bed instead. I've long since learned that I'm the weird one for wanting more than a physical connection.

When Carl continues, I'm glad I curbed the impulse. "When I say coffee, I actually mean coffee. So if you're expecting something else..."

"Nope!" I can't quite hide how nice that sounds. "No expectations, Carl. Coffee sounds wonderful, as long as it's with you."

"Phew. Let's go then." He squeezes my hand, rigid tension going out of his shoulders as he sidles closer to drop his head to my shoulder. We stroll toward his car hand in hand. The closeness makes me wonder what it might be like to snuggle even closer than that. Not sex...but would cuddling fall within his boundaries?

I wait until we're in the relative privacy of his car to ask. "I know you said no to sex. But kissing is okay. So, I'm wondering how you feel about cuddling? Or making out with our clothes on? I guess, just, where are the lines I shouldn't cross?"

"Cuddling is good." Carl glances over at me, mutters something I don't catch under his breath, and then he says. "I suppose at this point I should just tell you. I'm ace."

"Ace?"

"Yeah. Asexual. And that response is why I don't tell many people. They usually don't know what it means and unless we're dating, it's none of their business."

"But we are dating."

"*Fake* dating." He flashes me a rueful smile.

My stomach drops at the reminder that this isn't real. My feelings for him are anything but fake anymore. But he's right, and I just can't reconcile how a relationship with Carl could work once I'm back in Toronto. It's not like I have much vacation time for visits. It's already been a huge stretch to take most of December off to help Mom. My boss has been breathing down my neck about when I'll be back in the office to deal with a problem client who has been requesting me by name.

Nevermind that the time away has only made me realize just how much I dread going back to that office when this month is over. Other than my job, what do I really have waiting for me in Toronto? A lifeless ultramodern penthouse condo? A job that sucks out my soul and steals all my time? More failed superficial relationships that don't fulfill me?

"Right. Fake dating. So, what does it mean?" I ask.

"It means I'm not really sexually attracted to anyone," Carl explains. He combs the fingers of one hand through his bushy beard.

"So, when you said no casual sex, did you mean that, or just no sex at all?" I ask.

"Oh, no. I enjoy sex sometimes. It's just not something I crave most of the time or with most people. I'm more attracted to, well, what we've been doing. The sweet little shared moments of intimacy."

"If we were really dating?"

"Then coffee would still mean coffee. But if you wanted to sleep over, I'd like the idea of cuddling. It's been a long time since I woke up in someone's arms. Other than Saint."

"You two sleep together still?" I try to keep my tone neutral.

Carl fidgets his fingers on the steering wheel. "Sometimes? Not often anymore. It gives people the wrong idea. We aren't together romantically.

I wasn't lying when I said he's my best friend, but I do still love him platonically. And he loves me. It's complicated? This is another reason I don't do well with dating..." Carl blows out a loud breath.

"Guess we've got that in common. How did you figure it out?"

"Saint bought me a book about two ace men falling in love." Carl shrugs. "That's also how he figured out that he's aromantic. Meaning he doesn't really have romantic attractions, so our marriage was basically doomed from the start."

"I'm sorry." I want to comfort him at the pain in that wry observation, but I'm not sure how. He covers the emotional wound fast with a forced chuckle.

"It is what it is. We were making ourselves miserable trying to meet each other's opposing relationship needs. I crave all those little gestures that will never come naturally to him. Even when he tried, like with the cookies I told you about."

The sweet gestures that have so attracted me to him. All the little things like holding hands in the moonlight and kissing under the mistletoe, skating until the rink closed, nostalgic snowball fights among the Christmas trees, baking cookies together, and planning future dates. Picking out matching ugly sweaters earlier today for his sister's party tomorrow. Freezing our balls off to enjoy the light parade. All of it is so perfectly Carl and I want to know him more.

"Um. So it doesn't mean you hate sex?"

"No. Some people do, but that isn't me. I just don't care about it enough to pursue sex for its own sake when there are so many other things I'd rather be doing with a partner."

Those words flip a switch in my head. They slot into the part of me that has felt broken every time a new ex throws my lack of sexual interest into my face.

"Oh."

There's a word for how I've felt. For all the frustration and relationships that fizzled after a few promising dates. For the crushing disappointment when engaging conversations with a crush ended in frantic couplings. Sex that didn't do half as much for me as the anticipation of going to an interesting movie or a night of stargazing at the planetarium or almost anything else.

Carl flashes me a sad smile. "That's why this week has been so perfect."

"Um. Yeah. It's been perfect for me too. I think..." I lick my lips, not sure enough to actually say the words aloud. Am I ace like him? Except I want to have sex with Carl. I want our sweet kisses to lead to more. It's too soon to claim that identity for myself when I don't really understand what it means.

"You think?" Carl arches a brow at me as he pulls into his driveway to park.

"I really like you." I chicken out. Not ready to face the possibility that his label for his sexuality might fit me too.

"I really like you, too. Come in for that coffee?" Carl pulls the keys out of the ignition and smiles at me.

Damn, he's cute when he's looking at me with longing in his eyes. And it's even more enticing knowing that desire is unlikely to turn into lust overriding all our plans. That we can sit up for hours sipping coffee and discussing anything and nothing at all and it will all feel brand new the way everything has with him.

"Yeah. Coffee and cuddles. All night if you want." Please let him want that. It would be nice to hold him while he sleeps. To wake up tomorrow to his sweet smiles and even sweeter kisses.

"That sounds perfect."

Chapter 12

CARL—DECEMBER 23RD

I WAKE UP SLOWLY with the warm weight of someone's arms around me. "Mm, lemme up, Saint," I mumble into the muzzy predawn stillness of my bedroom. "Gotta pee."

If it was up to me, I'd snuggle here all morning, but my bladder has other plans so I squirm toward the edge of the bed. It's possible sharing a pot of coffee with Nick last night was inadvisable if I wanted to sleep in this morning. I freeze as the memory of coffee-flavored kisses before bed comes into sharp focus. It's not Saint's morning wood nestled against my back.

Not my best friend's familiar arms holding me. Not his sleep-gruff voice in my ear, sending pleasant tingles down my spine.

"I'm no saint," Nick says. Then he presses a kiss to my nape and rolls away from me. "But by all means, don't let me keep you from your business."

"Shit, sorry!" I scramble upright fighting the guilt at mistaking who he is. Worry roils low in my belly. Is Nick going to be less cool when confronted by the slip of my tongue versus just hearing there's another man I share my bed with on a semi-regular basis.

"Well, if you are shitting in the bed, you should be sorry." Nick widens his eyes comically.

"I didn't mean—" I flail in mortified frustration. It's too early to be talking.

Nick chuckles as he reaches up to put a gently shushing finger to my lips. "I know what you meant, babe. You told me you guys have sleepovers, it's fine. I'm not so insecure I can't handle sharing your affections as long as we're on the same page about what that means."

"We are. Saint is my platonic life partner, but he's not my boyfriend." I don't expect him to know what that phrase means and I'm not looking forward to the slew of questions, but it's broken more than one potential relationship before. Better to lay all my cards on the table.

"Good, because the boyfriend role is taken, at least until Christmas." Nick gives me a flirty wink, giving no sign my admission about Saint's role in my life phases him in the least. Is it possible that he's really this laid-back about it? He's still smiling.

Or maybe it's because this is temporary. That reminder shouldn't disappoint me as much as it does. "No need to explain a thing," he adds, watching my face. "Go pee. I'll still be here when you get back."

"Excellent, because I'm not done with you yet." I lean across the mattress to steal a quick kiss, determined to enjoy this easiness between us for as long as it lasts. Then I bolt for the washroom to take care of my morning ablutions.

I might take a few extra moments to brush my teeth if there's going to be kissing in my future. Not that I mind Nick's morning breath, but since I'm in there, might as well. It's been a long time since I wanted to impress someone this much.

When I return at a more sedate pace, Nick lifts the blankets in invitation and I slip in next to him. Nick rolls halfway on top of me and I tense at first, expecting him to push for more even though we talked about this. Disappointment weighs heavier on my chest than he does. I could cry from the frustration if it wouldn't be humiliating to waste my tears on something that was never meant to last.

It's just that I didn't expect Nick to push for sex. Not after he took my coming out so well last night. No overused jokes about invertebrate reproduction or clueless comments. Just genuine questions that were relevant to our context. Plus, he gave me that soul-searching look of such deep understanding that I have to wonder if he's known other ace folks without learning the label.

It is probably too much to hope he might recognize himself somewhere on the ace spectrum. Nick had so many questions over our late night coffee. I let myself cling to that slim hope. But if he thinks I'm suddenly going to want sex just because I invited him to share my bed, I guess he didn't truly understand. Instead of pressing the issue, Nick notices my response and eases back.

"Is this okay? I want to kiss you, but if you aren't into it, we can stick to cuddling?"

Or maybe he does get it. Maybe he's even more perfect than I thought.

"Kissing is good." I relax under him, letting myself enjoy the contact. Letting myself trust him not to trample over my boundaries. It shouldn't be so hard to believe a guy could respect who I am and be this into me. It still takes all my faith to lose myself in the moment with Nick.

Nick kisses me, then lifts onto one elbow to gaze adoringly down at me, and I find myself squirming at his intensity.

"You give the best kisses." Nick buries his fingers in my beard as he presses our lips together again in another lazy glide of our tongues.

He coaxes me into opening up to him and we lay there kissing in my bed until my lips are tingly from the scrape of his stubble. He eventually excuses himself to go open his mom's booth at the market for the second-to-last day of sales.

I get dressed to go with him and help since I know it's going to be a busy day. We share a companionable breakfast standing in my kitchen before we swing by Tina's on the way to the market for Nick to get ready. The market closes around the same time Eliza's party starts tonight, but my sister won't mind us being fashionably late. Especially since I'm bringing a date for her to gossip about. That was the entire purpose of this whole ruse, but at this point, I'm half-tempted to skip the party to keep Nick all to myself.

I wait in the car while Nick runs in to check on his mom and get dressed. I'm only putting off the inevitable inquisition from Tina about my intentions with her son until I see her again. Hopefully, by then I'll have the answers she'll want. All I know is that I intend to stretch out every moment we can steal together between now and his inevitable return to Toronto. We can figure out what happens after that when the time comes.

⋙⋙ ⋘⋘

"So, WHAT'S GOING ON with you and Hotty McHotness?" Eliza corners me by the punch bowl. Across the room, her wife has my fake date cornered, so this was definitely planned. All my sisters can be ruthless strategists when they put their minds to it. It's why I've long since stopped inviting them to the center's bingo nights and I only play cooperative board games with them at family get-togethers. I want all that evil genius on my side.

As my eldest sister tries to ferret out the family gossip, it feels decidedly like she's turning that tenacious streak against me. It's no use hiding the public parts from her, especially when I know our brother-in-law must have spilled about our tree farm date.

Marcus pretended to look the other way when we came back tousled and with damp patches on our clothing from playing in the snow. I'm not naïve enough to think he didn't notice and pass along the information. At the least he'd have told Gail, and she wouldn't have been able to resist sharing with Eliza and her wife, Grace.

"We're dating. It's brand new, so I don't want to jinx it." That's even a part of the truth.

I still don't want to share what I've got with Nick yet. It's like the holiday treats from long ago stockings that I used to hoard to myself. A little slice of perfection that can only be diminished in the sharing.

I'm not ready to tell my family about Nick. Which is ridiculous since the entire point of our fake dating arrangement was precisely this, having an easy lie for when they pried into my love life at the party. Now that it's here, Nick doesn't feel like a fake date and sharing him seems too personal. There's irony in that, but I'm too raw with all the emotions of the past few days to appreciate it.

"Well, early days or not, it seems safe to say you've got yourself a new patron saint."

"Huh?" That stings almost as much as a physical blow.

I rub at my chest. Is she implying I need to rely on a partner's patronage to support myself? I don't. Sure the early years of running Days of Grace were lean, but my elder care nonprofit is well established now. It brings in enough to fund our activities and pay myself and a handful of staff a living wage. I'm not raking in the riches, but that was never the goal.

Or is she saying Saint is replaceable? He's not. His place in my heart has never been in doubt and I have enough love to give to both Saint and Nick. They don't want remotely the same parts of me, and I love them both in unique ways—whoa, do I *love* Nick?

I'm certainly falling for him, but it feels far too soon for love to enter into things, no matter what romantic notions I have. I care about Nick and an unguarded part of my heart wants the sparks we've been nurturing to grow into the sort of romantic love I've been longing for. But it's too soon and there's too much stacked against us to call it love, right?

"You know, Saint Nick? Or Father Christmas, if you prefer." Eliza winks at me.

"I'm sure Nick's never heard that joke before." I roll my eyes at her. "And some of us don't call our partners *daddy*, you perv."

I lock eyes with Saint as I scan the crowd, looking for an escape. He's talking with Angel—Marcus's tagalong baby sibling has grown up since we moved home from the city. Their starry-eyed crush over Saint hasn't dimmed in the slightest, judging from their possessive hand caressing his biceps as they flirt. My bestie quirks an eyebrow at me, darting his gaze between me and Eliza as though offering a rescue.

I shrug and angle myself back toward Nick. I want him to be the one to rescue me, but that's unfair when Saint's the one who knows me and my family's quirks. And I don't need a rescue. It would just be nice. Wasn't that the whole point of bringing a fake date tonight? To keep my family from meddling too much, no matter how well-meaning they are.

"And some of us do, you prude." The worn moniker is more abrasive than usual, but Eliza is too focused on waving across the room at her wife and blowing her a kiss to notice. It's not like I didn't know that about their relationship. It might just have killed Eliza to try not calling her wife *daddy* in front of the rest of us for any length of time. Especially in the early days of their saccharine sweet relationship. It's none of my business to comment on their pet names for each other.

It's just that Gail and Eliza calling me a prude is another way I've always felt like an outsider with my sisters when we discuss relationships. They're so open about what they like and I just...haven't found the words to tell them I'm not a prude.

I just don't care that much about sex so it's always been weird to me how much they do care. How much they assume that since I'm a gay dude, I must be even more into sex than they are, because of course that's just the way things are.

"I'm not a prude. Some things are just private." I give a token protest, that at least takes the focus off of what's between me and Nick.

I wish I was the one standing in the corner with him, observing the room from the edges of the crowd of assembled guests. He smiles and offers me a cute little wave when our eyes lock. I know my entire face lights up at the happiness flowing through my veins like champagne bubbles when his focus is on me. That gorgeous, kind, successful man who dropped everything to care for his aging mother wants to be here with me. I must be doing something right. Even if it's not real and it can't last.

"See? That's exactly what I'm talking about!" Eliza snaps her fingers and points inches from my face, like I've just proven her point somehow.

"What?" I turn toward her, bewildered. Across the room Saint disengages from Angel and makes his smiling way toward Nick and my sister-in-law.

"I don't think I've seen you smiling this much since you brought Saint home as your hubby. Happy looks good on you, Carl."

I open my mouth to refute that, but she's probably right. I've been pining. Not for Saint, or what we tried to build together. That was never going to work when we were both trying to build something completely at odds with itself. The friendship we've nurtured since then fulfills us both, but I've still wanted the sort of partnership Nick has been playing at with me.

A boyfriend who will hold my hand at a party like this. Who grins as we arrive proudly wearing our matching holiday sweaters covered in cross stitch dinosaurs in Santa hats trimming a tree. A partner who will smile and kiss me when I bring over our drinks. And whose idea of a romantic Christmas present requires more thought than lounging naked under the tree with a bow around his dick.

"Thanks, Eliza." I swallow down the impulse to tell her it's not real. Confess that I asked Nick to be my fake date because of the pressure of anticipating this conversation. Not to mention all the future conversations it will spawn when she disseminates what I told her to our entire family.

My sister notices the dip in my mood. Her eyes narrow and her lips purse on some new accusation or question or something. Except a warm arm wraps around me and pulls me into Nick's side. He kisses my temple.

"Everything alright over here, babe?" Nick asks as I press his drink into his hands, then take a sip of mine to steady my nerves and buy time before I have to answer. Saint catches my eye and winks as he chats with Grace. Grace gestures at the smaller tree in the entryway that's covered in gift-wrapped ornaments for the swap later. Saint is probably bragging about how he's going to 'win' the swap. He's so infuriatingly sweet sometimes.

My heart swells with affection at the support from both men. Saint for taking the time to find out what I needed and giving it to me and Nick for being there for me.

"Yeah. I was just telling Eliza how we met."

Nick grins. "Carl came to my mom's booth at the Christmas Market to help Saint buy an ornament for the party tonight and then I spilled Carl's cocoa."

"And you offered to replace it." I break in grinning fondly at the memory of that first perfect date that inspired our plan to pretend.

"And you only agreed when I promised to drink it with you."

"So we went skating around the big tree and closed down the rink."

"And ended the night with a perfect goodnight kiss." Nick is gazing into my eyes like he did right before that first wonderful kiss. All the anticipation and hope brimming to the surface with promises of a future we can't have.

"Aw, you two are adorable. Sounds like the sort of first date story you tell your grandkids, bro." Eliza watches the two of us alternate telling the story with hearts in her eyes. Her excited hug almost makes me spill my drink and I feel hollow for lying to her. And because she's right. If it was real it would make for wonderful family lore. She's so genuinely happy for me it aches.

The moment breaks when Nick's phone rings. He dismisses the call, but whoever it is calls back again. And again. And then sends a text that has the blood draining from Nick's face.

"I, uh, have to take this. Work emergency." He kisses my cheek, sets down his half-finished cup of punch, and heads toward the entryway as he dials. He shrugs on his coat and goes out onto Eliza's front porch to make the call. I watch him pacing on the phone through her front windows.

I'm numb when Nick comes back inside and murmurs into my ear that he needs to head back to Toronto tonight. He spends the rest of the party distracted. As we do the ugly sweater contest and ornament swap, he keeps texting work colleagues. He's so caught up in shooting antsy glances at the door that the magic is gone.

I hate to do it, but I need to escape. Saint is our ride home, so as soon as he declares victory despite leaving the swap with a plain ceramic angel ornament that's totally not his style, I ask if he minds leaving early. He volunteered to be Nick's and my designated driver. Turns out we didn't need the precaution. Nick got the call from work early enough that he hasn't actually touch a drop of Grace's famous butter rum, Marcus's spiked farm fresh mulled cider, or Mom's eggnog. He's stone cold sober and already a million miles away as we leave before Santa brings out gifts for all the kids in attendance.

Nick doesn't even bother to come inside as planned back at my place. He says he's sorry, but he has to go. He'll be in touch when he can. And then he waves as he backs toward the curb where he left his car and drives away. Weird how the world blurs as his taillights disappear from sight.

Saint rubs my back comfortingly. "I'm sure he'll deal with whatever it is and be back."

"Yeah." I swallow down my disappointment, bitter as ashes. I know better. If his work is calling him back early, then that's it for us.

I don't have any illusions about Nick's priorities and where I rank. All the holiday lights are a blur of golden fractals when I turn to go inside. I have to blink away tears. A wild part of me wants to go after Nick and beg him to stay with me. But what would be the point? This was never real. Better to rip off the bandaid now.

Saint bundles me inside, where I can let my heart break in the privacy of my living room. I cry by the light of a Christmas tree that I'd hoped would illuminate Nick and I cuddling on Christmas morning. The wrapped presents, ready for my niece and the rest of my family when I see them tomorrow, are a hollow reminder that Christmas is only ruined for me.

Chapter 13

NICK—DECEMBER 24TH

IT KILLS ME TO leave Carl at his place after his sister's Christmas party. All I want is to go inside with him. If my boss hadn't made it clear that my job is on the line if I miss tomorrow morning's client meeting, I'd be angling to wake up in Carl's bed again.

Instead of another evening with Carl, I stop at Tim's for a Double Double on the way out of town and drive through the night back to my sterile condo. The spider plant on my fridge is the only spot of brightness in the place. It looks decidedly under-watered despite the automatic waterer I jammed into its pot before leaving for Mom's last month.

I don't have the energy to deal with my overnight bag, packed with starry-eyed hope that it would see me through a very different ending to my night. I fall exhausted into my bed and take in the glittering lights of the city laid out below me.

There was a time when that million-dollar view filled me with pride in my accomplishments. That first night after I closed on this place, I'd celebrated with a bottle of champagne. I'd shared it with a boyfriend who was more interested in what we could get up to between my high thread count sheets than taking in the stellar views. Let alone discussing our days.

Would Carl love these lights as much as the ones we'd strung onto my mother's tree together? I'll probably never know. A night spent pining for a man I can't have won't help me present a cogent case tomorrow. It's my job to help convince Mr. Sagun to stick with Merryman and Associates with his multi-million dollar ad portfolio.

Losing that account when we've been working on their 'Healthy New Year' ads for months would be a disaster. It seems ridiculous that he's threatening to pull the plug and refuse payment days before the campaign's intended Boxing Day debut.

That will mean litigation and it's a catastrophe in the making. It just figures the same project I killed myself to finish remotely is coming back to destroy my holiday plans. Word is that someone on my team set the wrong date for a social media post to go live. So this steaming pile of shit landed on my plate to deal with on the eve of a major holiday when I should be home with my loved ones.

The fact *home* conjures thoughts of Elk's Pass pulls me up short. Toronto has been my home for over half of my life. Yet when I think of the perfect holiday, all I can see in my mind's eye is Carl's bright smile as he plays his guitar in my mom's living room. His lips warm against mine in the lightly falling snow. A feast with all Mom's friends and her home cooking. Beatrice even brought over loaves of her fresh bread and delicious pies.

Since when has home meant Elk's Pass? Since when has putting work over my boyfriends threatened to tear out my heart? Maybe I'm getting old, or it's the middle-of-the-night bleakness of my cold and lonely bed, but it's hard to convince myself this is all there is to life. That I'll be happy in ten years' time if I keep on my current trajectory.

I sleep fitfully, wishing I had Carl in my arms like I did last night to settle me. I should be anxious that we might lose the account, but I can't bring myself to feel anything but numb about that. In five years, it won't matter. We'll have other clients, other crises to handle instead of building a life. It all seems so...empty.

Bright and early on Christmas Eve, my boss greets me in our nicest conference room. Jim provides quality coffee at least. Then we pitch our case to Mr. Sagun, the CEO of a major fitness brand. It takes all morning and an extravagant lunch at a Michelin-starred restaurant to smooth his ruffled feathers. My intel was right. Sagun is livid that one of the scheduled posts in his Boxing Day ad blitz went live three days early, revealing the details of his sale early.

Jim and I wine and dine him into sticking to our contract rather than litigating the alleged breach in confidentiality. It's absurd that he thinks it's a surprise for a fitness company to launch a 'New year, new you!' themed sale on memberships around New Year's Day, but he's the client.

I keep wondering what Carl is up to. If he'd enjoy the tiny portions of gingerbread spiced steak and parsnip puree or if he'd laugh at the pretentious meal. Mostly, I wish I was eating cookies with him instead of drinking hundred-dollar wine.

It's late afternoon when we shake on our amended deal. Then I have to call in my entire team from their well-earned vacation to spend the rest of Christmas Eve pulling together a miracle. We agreed to replace the compromised social media posts with a new, slightly updated, version of the client's artistic vision. This one includes an upgraded video montage ad package Jim promised him. Nevermind that it normally takes longer than one day to put that sort of promotional video together.

We work late into the night. My team pulls off a feat the likes of which I wouldn't have imagined possible if my boss had suggested it last night when he called me at Carl's sister's party. It's after midnight when we submit the revised ad that gets the thumbs up from our persnickety client.

My team toasts to a stressful job well done, then disperses to our various interrupted holiday plans. Those with family and partners to get back to can't leave fast enough. I stick around to shepherd the others out and lock up the office.

Several of the young singles on the team troop off to hit the bars to celebrate. I turn down the invitation to join them. As their manager, I suspect they'll have more fun without me anyway, though they make a show of disappointment. It just all seems so pointless.

They exit the elevator, taking their bubble of post-stress hilarity with them. I watch as the doors close on the festive lobby and my team. The elevator takes me down to the eerie quiet of the parking garage.

My car beeps when I unlock it, the sound loud in the cavernous emptiness that drives home how strange it is to be in the office today. I drive along slushy streets, as gray and lifeless as the superficial milestones of success that I've been measuring myself by.

I drive through a city being pelted with a hazy gray drizzle. The streets seem as deserted as they ever are in downtown. A few blocks out of the quiet business district, I find myself cruising through the more touristy areas, bustling with holiday merrymakers making the most of the night.

Nathan Philip's Square is lit up in technicolor and music echoes across the square as skaters glide past the massive tree that Carl mentioned enjoying. With a pang, I know there's only one place I want to wake up tomorrow morning. The vision I've cobbled together of what success looks like pales in comparison to the picture Carl has been painting with me over the past week.

I want to be there for my mom as she ages. Who knows how many more Christmases I'll have with her? Looking at what I have to show for twenty years of putting my career first is bleak. I don't want to wake up in twenty years and find myself all alone when I have a community in Elk's Pass that would embrace me. A life full of friends, family, and even a love that can last, if I'm lucky. Something built on a foundation of shared interests and putting the people who matter first.

I'd rather spend the rest of my mornings waking up next to Carl's smiling face than chasing the next vital project, the next huge promotion, a bigger, penthousier condo. That's what I've been chasing for years and all it's gotten me is lonely. Compared to the glimpse of what it might be like to go back to my roots, I'm not sure what I want anymore.

It's late when I get back to my condo, but my phone buzzes with another text from Mom asking if I'll be home tonight. I've had my phone silenced all day and there are several other missed messages. I'm struck by the overwhelming need to hear her voice. Like I'm a little kid again and she can solve all my problems.

Mom should be asleep, but I know her sleep schedule has been wonky between her recovery, pain, meds, and just everything. I text first to ask if I can call. My phone rings almost as soon as I hit send.

"Well, there you are! I was starting to worry. Carl said you went back to Toronto for a last-minute work emergency, but it's not like you to leave without so much as a text."

"Sorry. Mr. Merryman has been breathing down my neck to get back in the office all month. Last night he said if I wasn't here for the meeting today, I should probably polish up my resume. I didn't have a choice."

"Hm. I thought you were spending the evening with Carl?"

"That was the plan. Did you see him?" I bite back a barrage of needy questions. I'm aching to know how he seemed. Was he upset? Hurt? Pining for me half as much as I'm missing him right now? I doubt it. He has his family, Saint, and even my mom to lean on. I've got...my half-dead spider plant. And Mom on the other end of a late-night phone call. That's not nothing.

"I did. Beatrice brought me to the booth with the last of the crafts for the season when you didn't show up to get them this morning. Carl was there by himself. He said something came up for you. I tried calling, but your phone went right to voicemail, so I figured you'd be in touch when you could."

Shit. I totally forgot about my commitment to Mom's craft booth when I rushed off to deal with work. I might be an asshole for that. My job might be incompatible with not being an asshole. And that's not who I want to be anymore.

"How did it go?" Mom asks.

"Eh? We saved the contract. Probably. Pulled a dozen people in from their family time to make some changes."

Changes that don't matter and no one will remember in a few days, let alone years. But I bet Carl will remember how I ran out on my promises to him. Fuck. I pinch the bridge of my nose, wishing I could go back to last night and just turn my phone off before the party. Even if it meant waking up on Christmas morning without a high-powered job to go move back to Toronto for.

"How did the market go?" I ask to distract from my self-recriminations.

"Wonderful. Carl had to close up early since he sold everything and he even got me a few new commissions. Not quite as many as you, but I suppose that's why they pay you the big bucks at your firm, right?"

I try to force a laugh, but it comes out strained.

"What's wrong dear?" Mom asks, clearly worried about me. That makes me feel even worse because I didn't give my promises to her a second thought when I dropped everything for work yet again. I'm the worst. And I'm going to change that. Starting now.

"Nothing." I shake my head, negating the word even as I say it. "Just...would it be crazy of me to put in my notice and try my hand at freelancing from Elk's Pass?"

"Not at all. Is that feasible?"

"If I sell the condo and downsize my lifestyle a bit? I think so."

"Well, you're welcome to stay with me while you build your freelance portfolio, or whatever you need to do to make the move work."

"Are you sure?"

"Absolutely. What do you think? No hard feelings if you aren't interested."

"I need to crunch some numbers, but yeah, I'm interested." I'm interested in building a family in Elk's Pass with Carl. Decorating for all the Christmases to come with him. But that's getting ahead of myself. "Hey, is it raining there too?"

"No, not anymore, but we got enough freezing rain last night to melt all the snow. It's a shame. I hear the power is out west of town where Hydro One hasn't buried the power lines yet. If you're planning to come back, drive carefully. The roads will be slick with the temperature drop overnight."

"Shoot. Carl would have loved a snowy Christmas morning."

Then it hits me. I need to win Carl back, and what better way than with the sort of grand gesture that will make him swoon? I'm going to pull out all the stops to give Carl a perfect holiday memory, and then I'm going to grovel for his forgiveness.

"Say, does Beatrice's niece still manage the ski hill?"

"Yes, why?"

"Can you get me her number? Or is it too late to call? And I might need a little help from you."

"Of course." Mom says. There's rustling on the line, like she's moving around. "I'm sure she's still up. Susan is a night owl. But what's the rush?"

"I'm going to make a little holiday magic; I have a boyfriend to win back." And this time, I don't want there to be anything fake about it.

Chapter 14

CARL—DECEMBER 24TH

I DRAG MYSELF OUT of bed on Christmas Eve with a throbbing head and crusty eyes from last night. That's what I get for indulging in a crying jag last night. Nick's abrupt departure shattered all my dreams of a single perfect Christmas to remember. I shouldn't be devastated that he put his career ahead of a week-old relationship that was supposed to be fake, but I really thought there was more growing between us. Until he left like it was nothing.

As I rub at gritty eyes, it strikes me that with Nick gone, there's no one to run Tina's craft booth at the market. Nick might not be the man I hoped he was, ditching us at the drop of a hat like that, but Tina deserves better. Especially on the last day of the market.

So even though my head is pounding in my skull with all the implacable force of Niagara falls, I get up and go through the motions. I smile for the last-minute shoppers who are making their rounds of the market. I sell every piece that Nick left on display, replacing them with more of Tina's art from the plastic storage bins under the tables. My sale remain steady until there's nothing left.

Then I sell some more when Beatrice and Tina enlist Beatrice's niece, Susan, to bring over another several full plastic totes. Tina seems surprised to see me instead of Nick running her booth, but she mostly covers up her concern.

I let her know that Nick got called back to work. It strikes me as odd that he didn't call to let her know he was leaving town. I suppose that's what happens when you fall for a workaholic, you get forgotten and left behind.

A more charitable part of me realizes it was late when he left because he stayed with me until the end of Eliza's party. Nick probably didn't want to disturb his mother's sleep. He must be absorbed in his work now, but I assure Tina that her son will probably be in touch as soon as he can. She pats my hand, like she sees right through my optimism, and empathizes with my dashed hopes.

While Tina and Beatrice fuss over the displays and handle customers, I help Susan bring the empty totes back to Beatrice's car and the full ones to the craft booth. We chat about the abysmal weather and the dreary drizzle of rain that matches my mood.

"If this rain keeps up, it's going to make for a rocky start to the season. We're supposed to be open for tubing all next week while the kids are on winter holidays. At this rate, we won't be able to open even with the snowmakers," Susan says as we swap out the last few boxes.

"Fingers crossed the weather cooperates and all this drizzle turns to snow." I try to sympathize, but the gloomy weather matches my mood.

The unseasonable rain is depressing. It obliterated the dusting of snow that made me feel some kind of way about Nick. Was it really only two nights ago that we held hands through the light flurries dusting down on the light parade?

Tina and Beatrice stay to help run the booth for a few hours before I shoo them off to go warm up and rest. I sell almost everything. It makes for a busy day, but I'm glad of the distraction. The steady flow of customers keeps me from obsessing over Nick until I get home. I'm not sure how I'm going to get through the evening when I had so many half-formed hopes about spending tonight with Nick.

There's a perfunctory knock on my door shortly after I get home from closing down Tina's craft booth. Her display materials are all jammed into my car to deliver to her after the holidays. I can't bear to face her right now, when I'm so mad at her son. Anger and pining are a noxious cocktail in my belly, pushing me to the verge of tears or puking, or possibly both.

Saint doesn't bother waiting for me to respond to his knock before letting himself in. He must have been worried about me. After how last night ended, I'm not surprised.

He takes one look at me and opens his arms for a hug. I fall into his embrace and let the tears flow. Saint pats my back and mutters soothing nonsense into my hair.

"I thought he was different." I eventually pull back and swipe away the tears, angry at myself for getting so invested in something that was supposed to be fake.

"Want me to beat him up for you?" Saint jokes.

I know he doesn't mean it, but I still shake my head vehemently. A small part of me warms at the reminder of how deeply Saint cares, even if it's not in all the ways I once wished for. But a bigger part is horrified at the idea of him hurting someone else I care about. As if more hurts can somehow cancel each other out.

"No." I sniffle and try to laugh at myself, though it comes out as more of a broken sob. "It wasn't even real."

"Huh? You lost me, seemed pretty real when you were sighing over all those romantic dates you two shared. It was like a greatest hits reel from one of those lovey-dovey movies you adore."

I shake my head. "Yeah, that was the point. Remember how you said I should find a fake date for Eliza's party?"

"Yes. And you shot me down." Saint reminds me.

"Well, I reconsidered. I told you how Nick and I bumped into each other again as I was leaving the market?"

"Because you happened to wander back past his booth after we parted ways?" Saint gives me a teasing nudge and a suggestive lift of his eyebrows.

"Or because you happened to shove me toward his booth before you ditched me," I retort, flushing at the reminder of how I'd been drawn to Nick from the start.

"You're welcome; you love me." Saint puffs out his chest. He's right, I do love him, smug self-satisfied smile and all.

I hold my fingers up, pinched together but not quite touching. "Just a smidge. Anyway, we got to talking, and I explained about the party, and how nice it would be to have the whole boyfriend experience for the holidays, and he agreed. I mean, that he wanted to experience it too. And we figured since he was going back to Toronto in a few weeks anyway, there wasn't much risk of deeper feelings, so why not?"

Saint shakes his head at me. "Babe, I love you, but that is the second most boneheaded plan you ever came up with."

I shove him. "What's the first?"

"Marrying me." He kisses my temple and rubs my arms. "But that turned out alright in the end. This still might too; you're an easy guy to love."

"He left town without even telling his mom. I had to tell her at the market today when she came by her stall to see him."

"Sounds like his work-life balance sucks."

"Yeah."

"Are you going to go after him?"

"What? No!" My knee-jerk rejection of the idea seems to take Saint aback. I consider whether the love I was starting to feel for Nick might be worth fighting for, then shake my head. "No. I liked him a lot, and it hurts that he didn't reciprocate, or at least not enough to give me a second thought today. I get that work emergencies happen, but he didn't even call me. Or even his mom. *I* had to tell her he went back to Toronto. He warned me that his job is demanding, but I know better than to think love is enough to change a person if we aren't fundamentally compatible."

"We found a way to make things work," Saint ventures.

"Yeah, and everyone thinks we're weird as fuck, in case you haven't noticed." I gesture vaguely around us, taking in the shared duplex and the fact that my ex-husband is the one whose shoulder I'm sobbing on over my broken heart.

"If it makes things easier for you, I can give you more space to pursue other relationships." Saint offers, frowning. If I couldn't tell from his face that it kills him to offer me that, I'd be pissed.

"Nope." I shake my head and hug him tight. "No way. You're stuck with me."

Saint squeezes me back even as he sighs theatrically. "Guess we'll just have to keep searching for the right guy to get me out of those pesky alimony payments."

I roll my eyes. "I'm still not touching that money."

"Fine, it will be there if you ever need it. And someday, if it's still sitting there untouched, we can use it to fund our lavish retirement."

"Yeah?"

"Yeah." He nods decisively.

I resign myself to accepting I won't convince him to stop with that nonsense, but it's comforting to think we can always be close like this. Grow old together, even if it's not the way I'd envisioned when we said *I do*. I just really want there to be another man in that picture with us. One who can love me the way Nick and I were playing at. It's just too bad we pretended so well that I bought into the illusion we created with all those romantic evenings together.

Saint's phone rings. When he pulls it out to check who is calling, I see Angel's name on the caller ID. Saint goes to shove it back in his pocket, ignored, but I stop him.

"You can answer that."

"They want to come over because their ex has the kids tonight."

"All the more reason to answer. That's got to be hard."

Saint shrugs. "They're getting attached. Better not to lead them on."

"You've told them your stance on relationships, right?"

"Yeah."

"So, you're not leading them on. It's up to them to manage their expectations, but they could probably use a friend tonight."

"Sure, but so could you."

His phone stops ringing. Stubborn bastard. "So, invite them over and the three of us can make popcorn and watch cheesy movies together."

Saint sighs, but he pulls out his phone and calls Angel back to invite them over. Unlike most of my dates over the years, Angel doesn't seem the least bit put off by sharing Saint's attention with me. The three of us squabble over what to watch first.

Angel and I override Saint's protests that *Die Hard* is a Christmas movie and put on *Jingle All the Way* instead. It's not the Christmas Eve I'd hoped for, but cuddling on the couch with Saint and Angel eases some of the ache of Nick's unexpected absence. Funny to think someone I barely knew a week ago could leave such a void in my heart, but love is strange like that. Strange and sometimes cruel.

I'M DISORIENTED WHEN I wake up on my couch sometime before dawn. Is that bells ringing? And Christmas carols? I blink blearily awake and struggle free of Saint's arm around me. He mumbles a wordless protest. On his other side, Angel is snoring softly. Saint snuggles into them when I get up.

My television is glowing with the streaming service logo, long past the time when the 'are you still watching?' dialog box timed out. We must have fallen asleep in the middle of a movie.

The music is still playing. I go to the window and peer out to see what's going on. It's absurdly early for carolers. But that's not what I see. Snow. It's snowing perfect fluffy flakes that drift through the air and cover my lawn.

I rub at my eyes and take a closer look. Someone is standing on my front walk with a speaker playing music. No, not someone. *Nick* is standing in front of my house in a Santa hat and the ugliest Christmas sweater I've ever seen. The wobbly stitches and lumpy felt letters across the front don't spell the typical holiday greetings. Instead, it reads *I'm sorry.*

"Oh!" I stifle the exclamation with a worried glance at the couch. There's no reason to wake Saint and Angel. But this is like a scene out of one of the romances I've talked Nick's ears off about. Surely that means something? I try not to let myself overthink this as I shrug on a jacket and jam my feet into my boots.

As soon as I open the front door, the song changes to "All I Want For Christmas is You." Out here, I can see Susan standing in my driveway. She's got the snow machine from the ski and tubing hill she manages. She shoots me a thumbs up when I catch her eye.

And Nick walks up to me before dropping to his knees in the snow.

"What are you doing?" I ask, hands pressed to my chest over my heart that's beating fit to burst free of my chest.

"Winning you back. If you'll have me?" Nick reaches for my hands, and I let him cup them between his palms. "Carl, I messed up leaving here yesterday. Last night, driving past the skaters at Nathan Phillips

Square, I realized, there's so much more to life than a job that makes me miserable. I missed being here with you. I've missed out on so many holidays to climb the corporate ladder, but spending the last week with you showed me everything I've been missing."

"The magic of Christmas?" I suggest ruefully. I'm wary of trusting him again. He showed me his priorities, right? Except he's here now, and he put real effort into this apology.

He shakes his head. "Love. All the little things that make life worth living. Your smiles, cookies fresh from the oven. A house that feels like a home because it's full of memories and mementos of a life well lived. Music in the living room with Mom, taking the time to walk hand-in-hand. Connections that go deeper than the superficial, deeper than sex. Kisses that make me come alive. You." He licks his lips, adjusts his grip on my hands, and whispers, "I'm falling for you, Carl. I know we agreed to fake dating, and I messed up even that much by leaving. I'm more sorry than I can say for that. Can you find it in your heart to give me a chance to be your boyfriend for real? Let me learn to love you properly?"

I nod, too overwhelmed that he feels the same to voice an answer. And scared. He's saying all the right things, but what happens when his boss calls him home to Toronto again?

We have so many details to discuss, a larger conversation that needs to happen. But he came back to me. In the end, I matter enough for him to drive through the night to be back here with me. I want this. We can figure out how best to build our future together later.

"Yes?" Nick asks, his face shining with the same hope that fills my heart. I want to believe in him, and in us.

"Yes!" I nod, pulling him to his feet and into a kiss full of all the love in my heart that I thought I'd have to get over.

If Nick wants this as much as I do, we can make it work somehow. Just like Saint and I found a way to love each other after our marriage ended. I can visit him in the city, or he can try to work remotely sometimes. We can figure something out.

"Good." Nick grins against my lips. "Because I sent in my resignation before I left Toronto."

"You can't quit your job for me!" I swat at his chest, horrified at the weight of that, but also reassured that he's serious about refocusing his priorities.

Nick catches my wrists and tugs me more firmly into his arms. "I didn't. I quit for me. And I'm staying with Mom while I figure out exactly what's next for me. But whatever that is, I want it to be here, with you. I want to be happy."

It's a relief to hear that. All of it. The parts where it's not solely about me. That the sudden upheaval to his life isn't all on my shoulders. And the part where he is serious about trying to make a relationship work between us.

"You weren't before?" I ask.

"No. I didn't realize how unhappy the corporate grind made me until I came here and you gave me a taste of what happiness truly looks like. Now that I've sampled it, I can't go back to how I was living."

Nick kisses me again, with the homemade snow swirling around us in picture-perfect eddies. I melt into my boyfriend's arms, kissing him until a wolf-whistle from my front door breaks us apart. I grin when I see Saint standing there with Angel tucked under his arm, yawning.

Oh. I almost forgot I left Saint and Angel asleep on my couch. Will Nick mind that they slept over? Best to find out now. I glance between Nick and my overnight guests, but Nick just waves at them. "Merry Christmas. Sorry if I woke you," he calls as he fumbles with the music app on his phone to cut the noise from the speaker.

"Merry Christmas. I'll give you a pass since you just made all Carl's Christmas fantasies come true. But you better not make him cry again or I won't be so quick as him to forgive you again. Come back to my place to give the lovebirds privacy, Angel?"

"Yeah. That sounds good."

Angel flashes me a thumbs up when they catch my eye. I can't wipe the goofy grin off my face as I watch Saint cop a feel before guiding Angel to his door.

Nick glances between me and the two of them, but he doesn't ask what we were doing.

"Holiday movie marathon. We fell asleep," I explain anyway.

"I'm glad you didn't spend the night alone. I know you were looking forward to a cozy evening." He slings an arm around my shoulders and kisses my temple.

"I was. Come in, there's still time to wake up together on Christmas morning."

"Sure. Let me just make sure Susan is all set with the snow machine."

"Yeah. Okay."

Nick jogs over to talk to her. Susan turns off the snowmaker. She gets in the truck and drives off with the machine still on its trailer, leaving a pristine blanket of untouched snow covering my yard. Nick comes back over to me and we watch the glistening snow reflect the twinkling lights along my eaves for a long moment. The crisp night air has my nose and ears tingling with the chill.

"Ready for bed?" Nick squeezes his arm around my shoulders.

"Yes."

I take his hand and lead him inside and up to my room. We kiss, and for the first time in ages, I think that might not be all I want, but it's late and we're both exhausted. I let the impulse to rub my body against his pass.

Nick follows my lead until our kissing turns into snuggles. I fall asleep next to him as the first rays of dawn lighten the room with the promise of a bright new day. Hopefully, the first of many Christmas mornings that I'll wake up to this man in my life and my arms.

Chapter 15

NICK—DECEMBER 25TH

A BUZZING PHONE WAKES me from a sound sleep to light streaming across Carl's bed. I look at the clock and groan. Almost noon.

"Sorry, you can go back to sleep if you're still tired," Carl says, tapping a message into his phone before setting it on his lap.

"It's fine, Merry Christmas, babe." I kiss his cheek and he flushes, turning to kiss me properly.

"It is now. The merriest Christmas." Carl favors me with his full wattage grin. His phone buzzes again between us.

"Need to get that?" I ask through a yawn.

"Nah. I was just catching up on the family text thread. Eliza has been teasing Gail that it's her last year to sleep in, now that she's got a baby on the way. So she sent pictures of my niece—bright-eyed and begging for presents—around the time we went to bed. And Saint says we should get up and come over for brunch; he's given us enough time to sleep in."

My stomach grumbles, reminding me that the last thing I ate might have been gourmet, but it's been almost a full day since lunch with my boss and our client.

"I could definitely eat," I agree. "And Mom will be antsy for the play-by-play on whether you took me back."

"Did she help you make that sweater?"

"Yes? Sort of. She told me to let you know I made it all by myself with only a little help."

"It's good for a first attempt." Carl laughs.

I snort. "You don't have to sugarcoat it. I know my talents lie elsewhere."

"It's the thought that counts, Nick. Honestly. I love the sweater and that you thought of me and gave me the perfect apology to top off the perfect holiday season. I guess there are a few things we should probably discuss now that we're both awake?"

"Like what?" I ask. I have my guesses, but I want to hear his most pressing concerns before I spill my guts to him. The recent revelations he's helped me accept about myself are still fresh enough to be hard to put into words. Let alone to bring up out of the blue. It's easier to let him initiate this conversation, but I'm glad we're talking about it.

"Like how I'm not going to suddenly want to have sex all the time just because we're boyfriends. Sometimes I like it. I enjoy touching you and kissing, but sex is messy and awkward and not my favorite way to spend our quality time together."

"Good." I smile at the surprise on his face, eyes wide and lips parted, but really, that sounds perfect to me too.

If Carl hadn't mentioned being ace, I'd never have looked into it. He's shown me it's possible to have a connection this deep without compromising on my low libido.

I'm not sure that I would have ever admitted to myself that the label fits me if it weren't for him. Literally stumbling into someone who opened my eyes to something so fundamental about myself makes the two of us finding each other seem miraculous.

"Well, that's a first." Carl rubs the back of his neck, not quite meeting my gaze. "I can't tell you how many times that has been a deal breaker."

I shrug and nudge our legs together under the covers. "Well, it's a perk as far as I'm concerned. I've been thinking about it since you told me that you're ace. I did some reading. Turns out, I'm thinking I'm some sort of gray ace too. I've always been less interested in sex than most of my boyfriends. Before you, I didn't realize that it was even possible to find someone who feels the same way. It's validating knowing there's a word for this, and I'm not just weird for thinking there are better ways to connect. It's freeing not to have to weigh the pressure of meeting my partner's desire to have sex against being lonely. I've held back my heart for years, knowing my lack of interest would always become an issue, so this seems really special."

"It is special." Carl gives my leg a squeeze through the blankets. Our eyes lock and I could lose myself in the warmth of his gaze. It's like he really sees me past all my defenses. "I'm honored to be a part of helping you figure that out about yourself. We don't have to do anything you aren't comfortable with."

"Thanks," I choke out past the tightness in my throat. His words hit the center of my chest like a punch. I have to squeeze my eyes shut against the emotions welling up inside me. I've never given myself that permission before, and it brings stinging tears of relief to my eyes for that insidious pressure to be gone between us.

"Hey, it's okay. What's wrong?" Carl soothes me. His hand is warm on my back as he rubs a comforting circle while I try to gather myself.

"Sorry, just, no one's ever said that before. And I think I needed to hear it."

"Of course, baby. It's a big thing, huh?"

"Yeah. Huge. I'm really excited to explore what a relationship looks like between us, Carl. You make me feel so seen. I mean, I don't want to give you the wrong impression either. I like sex sometimes and I think I'd want it to be a part of our relationship, if you're open to that?"

"Me too. And I am." Carl leans in for a side hug. He brushes his lips over my temple. Touching me seems to comfort him as much as it does me. He pulls away to give me a soft smile. "As long as we both want it. Fair warning, I'm perfectly happy if sex only happens every few months, more often if we're both in the mood?"

Carl bites his lip, like he's bracing for me to disagree.

"That sounds perfect to me," I rush to reassure him like he just did for me. He couldn't be any more right for me, and I need him to know it.

Then I consider how to broach the other subject we need to discuss. How he spent last night in another man's arms. Or at least, Saint was sleeping at his place when I showed up. Not that I have any right to be mad that he cried on a friend's shoulder when I'm the one who made him sad. But he's made it clear that his relationship with Saint runs deeper than most friendships.

"I suppose we should also discuss how you're in love with Saint?"

Carl tenses at my side again, which isn't what I wanted at all. I give him a long moment to formulate a reply instead of rushing to clarify or talking over him. "I won't deny that I still love him. It's not the same way I'm falling for you." I can see his nerves as he clenches his hands together. "You should know that I wouldn't..."

I press a finger to his lips. "It's okay. I know. I also looked up queer platonic relationships—I guess people call them QPRs? And I'm still not sure I understand everything that means, but I support whatever is between the two of you." Carl's expression goes from incredulous to increasingly delighted, so I keep going. I always want to see him this happy. "Saint's part of your family, so I want to get to know him better. But I want you to know that I would never want to come between you guys."

"Saint would make that an innuendo about how he'd be perfectly happy to come between us, if we were into that." Carl sounds almost giddy with relief. He snuggles back into my side, like he can't help touching me. I'm totally on board with all the cuddles he wants to give me. "So, you're good with Christmas brunch with Saint? And, I mean, I spend a lot of time with him."

I kiss his cheek. "Yeah. The holidays are for family, and I understand that he's part of the one I'm hoping we can build together. I'm not jealous of the time that you spend with your siblings or parents, so why would I be jealous of the time you spend with him?"

"How are you even real?" Carl asks. I know I made a dramatic show of my affections last night, but somehow, I'm thinking this was an even bigger Christmas gift.

"Oh, I'm plenty real. Believe me, you don't want to smell me right now." I make a show of sniffing my pits. "I stink after yesterday."

"You don't. I've been cuddling, so I would know. But I'm sure it was a long day."

"You have no idea. I'm not going to miss my job once the move is final. I just want to wash the stress away."

"Sounds good." Carl hesitates before asking, "Can I join you in the shower?"

He fidgets adorably with the blankets.

"You want to get naked with me?" I tease, gently clasping his fingers.

"Yeah." Carl turns his hand palm up to give me a squeeze. "I really do."

Chapter 16

CARL—DECEMBER 25TH

FOR ALL THAT A shared shower was my idea. I'm nervous as I follow Nick into my washroom. I hover in the doorway, watching him in my space. He's still wearing last night's apology sweater. The hastily appliqued letters are even more endearingly crooked in the light of day. I step closer to trace his sloppy 'S' with one finger.

"We can take turns in the shower if this is too fast." Nick gives me a reassuring smile.

"It's not that." I'm just not quite sure how to go from standing here in our clothes to naked under the water without it being awkward.

I edge past Nick to turn on the shower. It's not just a top-tier avoidance tactic; my shower always takes a few minutes to get warm. Saint keeps saying we need to update the old hot water heater, but I never get around to it. I'm stalling and Nick is standing patiently in the middle of my washroom.

I take a deep breath and face him. "What now?"

"Now, I want to unwrap you," Nick gently nudges the door shut to trap the shower's warmth. Then he leans in for a kiss, giving me plenty of time to take this in a different direction, but kissing him is perfect. He makes me feel like the precious gift his words imply he sees me as.

I love the way our lips meld together. His arms encircle me in a warm sense of belonging. I remind myself that Nick won't be upset if this doesn't go further than a kiss and an actual shower. Being on the same page about that makes all the difference. I press myself against him, and work my hands up under the soft green wool of his sweater.

"Mm, you can take it off for me," Nick pulls away from my lips to offer.

I slide my hands up his back, stripping him bare. Yet somehow, I'm the one who feels exposed as I take in more of his naked skin. He's just as nice to look at with his clothes off. By now I know better than to expect a rush of libidinous longing at the sight. But the way he smiles at me sends warmth rushing through me anyway.

Nick draws me in for another lingering kiss as he helps me out of my clothes. We fit together. He brings the spark of romance I've been longing for into my life. We undress each other between more tender kisses that make me feel cherished. My mirror is covered in a sheen of fog by the time we step into the shower together.

"Can I soap you up?" Nick asks, looking between me and my wash cloth.

I swallow hard at the intimacy of that gesture, and then nod, trusting him with a level of closeness I've only ever shared with Saint before. "Yeah."

Nick understands my boundaries. I trust him not to push past them. His hands are gentle as he rubs suds into my skin. His touches transcend anything sexual. It's like he's distilled down the essence of what it is to care about another person and is pouring it over me along with my body wash.

When he gets to my dick, he pauses, meeting my gaze with a question in his warm eyes. I take his hand and guide the warm slippery cloth over myself, body responding to the friction and heart full of love for this perfect man.

Nick's breath hitches when I move into the touch, pulling him closer. I want to delight in every part of him, the same way his every touch shows how much he adores me. He follows my lead as I pull him close.

I realize that he's aroused too, our erections bumping awkwardly together. "Is this okay?" I whisper. I get the impression Nick would agree that checking in is sexy.

"Yeah. I'm um... Well, you can see it." We both look down, and then he returns to my eyes. "I'm happy for this to go anywhere you want it to. We can just get clean, or we can see where this goes."

I run my hands down his chest, enjoying the closeness. The way his eyes never stray from mine, letting me see how he's leaving all his stress behind and committing himself to me again.

With adoration in my heart, I wrap my hand around us both. It's lazy and close. Like cuddling but a little more. Nick kisses and holds me as making out under the warm spray of the shower leads to making love. The sound of him coming with my name on his lips is as sweet as the cookies we made together. Nick keeps holding me as I follow him a few moments later. I can see myself building forever with this man in my arms.

"Mm, that was nice," Nick kisses my neck as he reaches for the forgotten washcloth..

"Yeah," I agree, still a little punchdrunk from coming.

"Want to help me clean up?" Nick offers me the washcloth. I try to be as tender soaping him up as he was with me. We finish getting clean and turn off the water. I dig out fresh, fluffy towels for us both.

"Was that alright?" Nick asks. "Not too much?"

Yeah, checking in is nice, and getting that from him warms me almost as much as the hot shower. "Just the right amount. Like the massage just kept going, but it was still romantic. And, added bonus, not too much clean up."

Nick chuckles. "It was good for me, too. Relaxing instead of stressful."

I nod in agreement. "I think we could do this again. And other things. Not, like, soon, but sometimes?"

I smile hopefully at Nick, and he beams back at me. I'm so warm and loose in the steamy confines of the bathroom. There's something so intimate about sharing this space that's usually so intensely personal with him that makes it easier to discuss other personal matters.

"That sounds good. It's really nice to know I don't have to justify why I'm not into sex all the time with you. I didn't realize how much that usually stressed me out with past relationships," he confides, and I could used to being the one he bares his heart with.

"Same," I chuckle. The relief of that basic compatibility is a palpable burden off my shoulders. That leaves only one major hurdle to building my happily ever after with Nick. He already said he's ready to embrace Saint's place in my life, but I just need to hear the words again. That I can love them both is music in my ears. I need him to confirm I wasn't just hearing what I wanted when we were talking in my bed.

"And speaking of exes, are you *really* okay having Christmas brunch with Saint?"

"Yeah. More than okay. This is the start of our own family traditions, right? He's more than your ex. I can't claim to have a similar experience, but Saint and I have loving you in common. We'll figure out where we both stand with each other and make it work."

It's a thrill to hear him just casually remind me I'm loved. I've fallen so hard for this man in front of me. This time when he says he's more than fine with Saint and me, I decide to believe him. I lean into the giddy euphoria of being able to have it all.

We get dressed and go over to Saint's together, foregoing coats and scurrying across our shared porch.

I'm surprised to see Angel at the door wearing Saints pajamas. Normally, Saint would mention having a guest over. In fact, bringing Angel into our Christmas celebrations seems like a big deal. Maybe not the same as Nick joining me, but Saint doesn't do relationships or romance. Our holiday traditions are usually just ours. Well, mostly mine with Saint joining in and humoring what a giant dork I am about bringing the holiday magic, but still... This is big.

He could just be giving Angel somewhere to go for the holiday, but I get the sense that there's something a little more going on. I give him an inquisitive look, but he acts baffled. Idiot. Maybe he doesn't see it, or he's just not ready to share what's between them. That's fine. I'll be here for him whenever he's ready, just like he was there for me.

I get to spend the afternoon with people who make me smile until my cheeks hurt. New love and old, sharing a table as Nick falls into easy conversation with Saint. I take the time to get to know Angel, a true sweetheart who seems to be increasingly important in my best friend's life. Our lives might be changing, but I know our love will endure.

I joke that this is our first annual family holiday brunch. Saint kisses my cheek and hugs my boyfriend when we leave to go to Tina's house. We wish Saint and Angel a Merry Christmas while I nurture the hope that the four of us can share many more brunches like this in the coming years.

Chapter 17

NICK—DECEMBER 25TH

"WE SHOULD GET GOING." Carl says, then immediately back peddles, adorably flustered with his hands flailing. "I mean, if you want to come back to my place with me, Nick?"

We've been at my mom's house for hours now. Beatrice and several of Mom's other friends came over for a big holiday feast and to exchange gifts. Carl and Bea are the only remaining visitors, which is probably fitting. Bea is in the kitchen getting another plate of cookies. So it's just my mom and my boyfriend sitting in the glow of the perfect tree we decorated together, enjoying the holiday afterglow.

"I'd love to," I smile at Carl and take his hand. He relaxes into his seat again. "Unless you need me to stay over? I can make sure you have your meds and everything..."

Mom welcomed us into her home with hugs and all her usual verve, but I can tell from the tightness around her smile that her hip is bothering her. She needs to go rest soon.

"Psh, don't you fuss over me." Mom flaps her hand at me, waving away my filial concern. "Beatrice is staying over tonight anyway."

I manage not to splutter when I put together the fact that my stuff is still in the only other guest bedroom. There's no way Mom would have her octogenarian best friend sleep on the couch, no matter how spry Bea seems. She wouldn't even hear of me sleeping on the couch when I first arrived at her house to find my bed covered in crafting supplies.

"Great, that's, uh, great?" I probably shouldn't be so surprised, and I cringe internally at myself for feeling like a kid who just realized that his teacher exists outside of the classroom. It's totally reasonable that my mom has an active love life.

I'm happy about anything that makes her happy, but I really don't want to think about her sleeping with anyone. Least of all the aunty I've always admired with a fond exasperation for the misadventures she and my mother get into together. The recent rollerblading incident that landed Mom in the hospital is only the latest in a long history of their exploits, and it's one of their tamer stories.

They met at a Roller Disco night in Hamilton and spent years meeting up at the rink every week until one opened in Elk's Pass shortly after Mom moved here. Bea helped me convince mom that nursing an orphaned fawn her late husband found on their farm back to health would build character when I was nine. She let me sleep in her barn to take care of round-the-clock bottle feedings. Bea consoled me when I sobbed over the little deer going to an animal reserve months later. I grew up viewing her as a second mother figure.

Bea and Mom have always been so close; I never noticed their relationship changing. Or maybe they've just always loved each other. In retrospect, it makes perfect sense that they're together. But I'm still gaping at my mother, mouth moving with no sounds coming out, shocked at the revelation. Carl rubs my back reassuringly. At least it makes more sense why she was so quick to provide me with Susan's number in the middle of the night. Beatrice was probably here and knew her niece's holiday plans.

"I take it you didn't know they're together?" Carl asks with a hint of wry amusement. For a second it stings that he knew already, but he's friends with them and I haven't been around. I'm glad I already resolved for that to change. I want to be a part of my mom's life. And Bea's.

"Did you tell the boy yet, Tina dear?" Beatrice comes back in with the tray of sweets. She looks between my dropped jaw and Mom's pursed lips as she tries to hold back a laugh at my shock.

"Not yet. I was getting to it. These things take delicacy, Bea." Mom's face is glowing at the sight of Beatrice though. "Look, he's shocked that I've still got it."

"Mom!" I groan, even though she's right and I'm being silly.

"Nonsense." Bea turns to me. "Nick, I'm sure you have questions. Your mother is moving in with me. We weren't together when your father and my Robert were alive. I can't speak for your mother, but I loved my husband dearly. He always said he wanted me to love again after he was gone." She takes Mom's hand in hers, gazing adoringly at her. I can only hope I'll still be looking at Carl with that much open admiration when we're their age. "Tina was the first great love of my life; it seems fitting for her to be the last too."

Then she kisses my mother.

I'm still staring, slack jawed, when Mom turns to me, eyes all aglow. She swats playfully at Beatrice. "You broke him, you ridiculous woman."

"Tell him the rest?" Bea nudges Mom. "You've been putting it off all month."

"I was just waiting for the right time."

"Mhm, not at all afraid he'd refuse? Well, Nicky already told you he's moving home. What better time than Christmas to give these boys a gift?" Beatrice gestures between Carl and me.

"What gift?" I ask. "Mom, you don't have to get me anything else. I love the new sweater."

"I want to give you the house." She holds up a hand to forestall the protest that forms on my lips. "Either way, it's time to downsize. Now that the cat is out of the bag, there's no sense beating around the bush. I'm moving in with Bea. She's closer to all the amenities and our friends."

"So you'll have to host craft night," Beatrice interjects with a nod toward Carl.

"That would be my pleasure," Carl agrees with a smile.

"I'm not sure what to say, Mom. I can't just accept your house." Even if selling my condo means I could probably afford to pay her market value for it. My vague notions of moving back in with Mom for a while longer to figure out my next career steps made it seem like I could change my mind. It gave me the safety net of going back to my big city grind if the lure of small-town life isn't so shiny once the newness wears off. This would make the change real. Less revocable.

That should terrify me, but I just feel more settled than ever in my decisions. I want to be here for Mom. Build a new career that gives me the flexibility to enjoy my life. Maybe get back into the digital design and photography that first drew me to the field. I can buy the house and still have savings to live on until I get myself established as a freelancer. And I can make the time to be the boyfriend Carl deserves.

"You can buy it then." Mom rolls her eyes, as though I'm being stubborn for not just accepting such an extravagant offer when she needs the equity from the house more than I do.

"Carl, your Saint does contracts, right? He'll arrange it," Mom says like that settles the matter. I'm not sure that's how these things work, but I don't really want to argue with her. "You boys can raise your family here."

"Saint does real estate contracts sometimes. He jokes that he moved back here so work would never be boring, since his clients have such varied legal needs." Carl's smile looks tight as he nods.

It takes me a second, but then I suspect I understand why. Saint. I just reassured him this morning that I don't want to take anything away from their relationship. And now here's Mom unwittingly undermining that assurance with her plans to move us in together before we've been dating for a full week.

"Or we can sell this place and move into Carl's when that time comes. I don't know that we need so much space for the two of us. Either way, I'm sure we'll want to stay close to Saint."

Carl beams at me, his arm around my waist tightening in a hug. I got it right. And while I have many happy memories of this house, my boyfriend and his platonic partner have been living together for over a decade. I can't take that away from him. We can make new memories together.

"Oh, of course, dear. I just want my boys to be happy." Mom winks at Carl as she reaches out to pat my cheek. "We can work out the details later. I just want you to know you have a place to live for as long as it takes to make your career change."

"Thanks. I appreciate your support Mom." I get up and hug her tight, then I turn and hug Bea too. Carl gets in on the love-fest too, hugging my mom and the woman who has always been another mother figure for me. "And I'm happy for you and Bea, truly. I hope you didn't think for a second I wouldn't accept you two."

"Of course not. I just wanted to tell you in person, and then I had the accident and it just never seemed like the right time. You will always have my support, my dear. I am so proud of you," Mom murmurs that last against my cheek as we embrace. Then she holds me at arm's length. "And now I really should get to bed. Lock up when you leave?"

"Yeah, of course. Good night, Mom. Merry Christmas." I kiss her cheek.

We all exchange more goodbyes. Bea tucks a stack of napkin-wrapped cookies into Carl's hands for later. Then she brings Mom her walker to help her get to bed.

Just as Mom and Bea head down to the hall toward Mom's room, Bea calls one more parting remark.

"Just know that if you boys have any children, I call dibs on being called their Gigi."

"Bea! Don't badger the boys," Mom protests, though her shoulders shake with suppressed laughter at Bea's audacity.

"I wouldn't be your honey badger if I didn't badger them a little. Anyway, I'm just saying, I'm the hip grandmother."

"Oh really? Then why am I the one with a bionic hip, Beatrice? Hmm?"

Bea snorts. "Pfft, I can get a newer hip. Just watch me."

"Please don't!" Carl, Mom, and I all protest at the same time.

Beatrice cackles with laughter. "Merry Christmas boys."

"Merry Christmas. Come on, Nick, I think we've overstayed our welcome." Carl tugs me toward the door while I try not to think too hard about my mom's love life.

Back at his place, I curl up on his couch to bask in the glow of his tree with a pot of coffee and some cookies. Carl gets the ornament mom made for us, two of her bright red felted cardinals snuggled together on a branch, and hangs it front and center on his tree.

"What do you think?" He gestures at the ornament.

"It's perfect, baby." I pat the couch and lift the edge of the blanket for him.

"So, back at your mom's place, you said we could move here together someday. Did you mean that?" Carl asks as he settles next to me, chin propped on my shoulder and arms around me.

"It's early days yet, but yeah. I promised I wouldn't come between you and Saint. I understand that means any major plans we make include him in our life, right?"

"Right. I just didn't want to assume you'd always want to live next to Saint." Carl forces a weak smile, as if this isn't a huge deal for him. I know it matters more than he's letting on.

"Well, if that's what makes you happy, then it's exactly what I want, Carl. I want to spend every Christmas from now on making you happy."

"I am." Carl kisses me, and I melt into his warmth.

We spend the rest of our first Christmas together watching cheesy movies by the soft glow of the tree lights. Carl's place is festive and inviting. It's everything that my condo in the city isn't, and Carl is everything I want for my future. I couldn't imagine a happier holiday than this.

***

Thanks for reading Carl and Nick's story! If you enjoyed it, I'd love if you would leave a review or rating to help other readers find this book . And if you're looking for more holiday magic, be sure to check out Angel and Saint's book, Christmas Angel.

For all the latest news about my sales and new releases, be sure to subscribe to my newsletter:

Other Works by Alex Silver

Merry Exmas

CONTEMPORARY CHRISTMAS ROMANCE

Christmas Carl (M/M) #1

Christmas Angel (M/X) #2

Table Topped

Contemporary Romance
 Roll for Initiative (M/M) #1 Gui & Paz
 Charisma Check (M/M) #2 Theo & Jude
 Saving Throw (M/X) #3 Errol & Rene
 Plus One Bonus (M/X) #4 Max & Si
 Dump Stat (F/F) #5 Laura & Alice
 Party of Three (M/M/X) #6 Pia, Emil, & Gregor
 Balanced Party (M/M/X) #7 Pia, Emil, & Gregor

Summer of Adventures

Kinky Contemporary Romance
 Dungeon Master (M/M)
 Knotty Boy (M/M)
 Service Call (M/M)
 Picture Perfect (M/M)
 Puppy Love (F/X)
 Stud Muffin (M/M/M)

Hauntastic Haunts

M/M Paranormal Romance
 Dan's Hauntastic Haunts Investigates:
 Goodman Dairy *Book 1*
 Hawk Lake *Book 2*
 Ivarsson School *Book 3*
 Joliet Asylum *Book 4*
 Kapler Hotel *Book 5*

Free download links to the shorts are available in my FB group:
Drew's Haunted Hangout (*A Hauntastic Haunts Short Story 1)*
Rafael's Haunted Halloween (*A Hauntastic Haunts Short Story 2)*
Lee's Haunted Holiday (*A Hauntastic Haunts Short Story 3*)

Shift Work

Omegaverse MPreg Romance
Papa Bear (M/X)
Squirrel Trouble (M/M) (expanded edition)
Trash Panda (M/M)

Psions of SPIRE

Urban Fantasy
Shelter (M/M) Novella 0.5
Bright Spark (MMMM)Book 1
Bold Move (MMMM) Novella 1.5
Keen Sense (M/M) Book 2
Weak Link (M/M) Novella 2.5
Quick Fire (M/X) Book 3
Clear Sight (M/M) Book 4
New Look (M/M) Novella 4.5

A SPIREverse daddy kink standalone
New Ground (M/M/X)

Shared Universe Series

Super U - Superhero Romance
   Super U: Rising Storm (M/X)
   Final Days - Zombie Romance
   The Willows (M/M GNC)

Anthologies

Listen: The Sound of Fear
   Haunt (M/M trans gothic horror)
   Fix the World
   Upgrade (gay trans cyberpunk)

About the Author

ALEX SILVER (HE/THEM) GREW up mostly in Northern Maine and is now living in Canada with one spouse, two kids, and a lovebird. Alex is a trans guy who started writing fiction as a child and never stopped. Although there were detours through assisting on a farm and being a pharmacist along the way.

Visit me online at:

http://alexsilverauthor.wordpress.com/

Browse my entire book catalog at:

https://www.amazon.com/Alex-Silver/e/B07NPBW615

Join my Facebook group at:

https://www.facebook.com/groups/alexsalcove

Follow me on BookBub at:

https://www.bookbub.com/profile/alex-silver

Follow me on Twitter:

https://twitter.com/asilverauthor

Sign up for my for a free short story at:

And as always, consider leaving a review on Amazon or Goodreads if you enjoyed this book, reviews are of vital importance to independent authors, thanks!